"M⟩ ⟨ ⟩ffered a
sym⟨ ⟩nd, and
you⟨ ⟩r two."

"We'll see." Brian stepped away from them and waved. "I'd better go talk to some folks and thank them for coming to the party that didn't happen."

Kim and David watched Brian until he disappeared into the crowd; then David casually placed his hand in the small of Kim's back. "I wouldn't wanna be Brian now." He gave her a squeeze. "But he seems to be handling it well."

She pulled away and studied David's profile—handsome in every way, from his deep-set eyes to his strong chin. "What choice does he have?"

"Huh?"

"You said he was handling it well. What else would a guy in his place do?" Kim paused and gave him a moment to think before adding, "What would you do if I stood you up at the altar?"

He gave her a mock look of shock. "That's not something I'll ever have to worry about, is it?"

Kim shook her head. "No, of course not."

David turned her to face him and placed a hand on each of her shoulders. "That's my girl."

DEBBY MAYNE has been a freelance writer all her adult life, starting with slice-of-life stories in small newspapers then moving on to parenting articles for regional publications and fiction stories for women and girls. She has been involved in all aspects of publishing—from the creative side, to editing a national health magazine, to freelance proofreading for several book publishers. Her belief that all blessings come from the Lord has given her great comfort during trying times and gratitude for when she is rewarded for her efforts.

Books by Debby Mayne

HEARTSONG PRESENTS
HP625—Love's Image
HP761—Double Blessing
HP785—If the Dress Fits
HP789—Noah's Ark

Special
Mission

Debby Mayne

Heartsong Presents

I'd like to dedicate this book to my editors, JoAnne Simmons and Rachel Overton, for all their time and attention to the details that helped make this book as good as it can be.

A note from the Author:
I love to hear from my readers! You may correspond with me by writing:

Debby Mayne
Author Relations
PO Box 721
Uhrichsville, OH 44683

ISBN 978-1-60260-709-5

SPECIAL MISSION

Our mission is to publish and distribute inspirational products offering exceptional value and biblical encouragement to the masses.

PRINTED IN THE U.S.A.

one

Kimberly Shaw stared up at the bridal party, imagining herself getting ready to walk toward her own adoring groom, David. The wedding singer's voice echoed through the small chapel as the groom and his men stood in a line, waiting. Her heart hammered. This would be her in less than a year—at least that's what she hoped.

After the singer finished her song, the chapel grew quiet for a few seconds. The organist positioned herself on the bench and opened her music book. A soft murmur started at the back of the church, but Kim figured people were just getting impatient. The wedding was running behind by—she took a quick look at her watch—about fifteen minutes.

She glanced back up toward Brian's guys. His smile had faded, and David leaned over to whisper something. Then suddenly Brian's mother scurried up the aisle and spoke to the pastor.

The murmur behind Kim grew louder. She squirmed in her pew. Something was happening; she just wished she knew what it was.

"Where's the bride?" Kim asked. "This isn't good."

"Oh, I'm sure it's nothing serious. I bet Leila couldn't get into her dress," Kim's best friend, Carrie, whispered. "Did you see her putting away two desserts last night at the rehearsal dinner?"

"Shh." Kim couldn't help but smile. "Yeah, I noticed. I don't know how she could eat the night before her wedding."

"Maybe she was nervous-eating. I do that with brownies." Carrie smoothed the front of her skirt.

Kim was about to comment, but the pastor returned to the front of the church. He whispered something to Brian, who hesitated, nodded, and tightened his jaw. The frown on his face deepened as he huddled with David and the rest of the guys, who all groaned then turned and headed for the side door.

"What is going on?" Carrie said. "You don't think we're taking this outside, do you? I hope not. These heels are hard enough to walk in on hard floors. There's no way I'll be able to walk in grass."

Kim nodded toward the pastor, who held up his hands to quiet everyone. "Folks, there's been a change of plans. There will be no wedding today."

Loud gasps resonated through the sanctuary.

"This is weird," Carrie said.

"C'mon." Kim scooted out of the pew and into the aisle, where a smattering of guests had already begun to congregate. "Let's go find out what happened."

"But—"

Kim didn't wait to hear what Carrie was about to say. After figuring out she'd have to deal with a crowded narthex, she turned and half walked, half ran up the front and out the side door. David held his cell phone up to his ear and paced. Brian leaned against a concrete wall by the fellowship hall, a stunned look in his eyes. Kim hesitated for a moment before heading toward David. He glanced at her and shook his head, the straight line of his mouth letting her know that something awful had just happened.

She turned toward Brian whose gaze locked with hers. Dread flowed through her, but someone needed to be with Brian, and all his friends stood several feet from him—as if they were afraid of him.

He'd always been there for her, no matter what. The least she could do was find out what happened and comfort him if needed.

Kim slowly moved toward him and forced a sympathetic smile. He remained fixed to one spot.

"What happened?" she asked as she reached for his hand.

"She changed her mind."

They stared at each other a couple of seconds while Kim's mind wrapped around what he'd just said. "I'm so sorry, Brian. I don't get it."

Brian's shook his head. "Yeah, I don't either."

"Can I. . ." Her voice trailed off as she tried to think of something to offer, but nothing came to mind. "Is there anything I can do?" She squeezed his hand. He didn't budge from his position.

"Not really. I'll be okay after the shock wears off."

"I'm sure," Kim said. "Have you talked to Leila?"

"Nah. She didn't have the decency to tell me. I knew she was late, but that's pretty normal for her. Her mom called my mom."

Kim wanted to shake Leila until her teeth fell out for doing such a rotten thing to such a sweetheart of a guy. "Would you like for me to try to talk to her?" If she'd been better friends with Leila, she would have talked to her without asking.

"Wouldn't do any good," he said. "Once Leila sets her mind on something, it's a done deal." He finally shifted, pulled away from her, shoved his hands in his pockets, moved a few inches from where he stood, then let out a sardonic chuckle. "In fact, she's the one who finagled the proposal."

"Yeah, I remember David telling me about that."

Brian pulled his hands out of his pockets and lifted them. "I was perfectly happy with the way things were going, but after you and David—well, you know, after she saw your ring and all. . ."

Kim held out her left hand and gazed at the sparkling diamond David had given her. After he proposed, she thought things would be wonderful—that they'd get married a few months or even a year later; then they'd live happily ever after. She had no idea that what started out as his part-time career with the National Guard would take precedence over their relationship. Shortly after they got engaged, he let the law practice he'd inherited from his father slide in favor of his passion for the National Guard. The patriotism she'd seen when they first met had become a source of contention between them.

"Sorry," Brian said. "David told me you're getting frustrated about having to wait."

"I'm just glad he's stalling now," she replied. "Before we get married."

"Just don't rush things," Brian said. "Look where it got me."

Except Brian wasn't the one who'd rushed the wedding. Leila's fantasy of the romantic wedding and honeymoon had been the topic of her conversations with all their friends for the past couple of months. David had even accused Kim of being like Leila when she tried to press for a date.

"Did David tell you he's thinking about volunteering to go overseas? For some kind of top secret special mission. Only a few select people from his unit will be involved."

Brian's forehead crinkled as he gave her a look of concern. "Kim, he's already been accepted." He gestured toward David who was still on his cell phone. "In fact, he's talking to his commanding officer right now. Before we got to the church, he said he needed to contact him before the day was over, so I told him to go ahead and call."

Kim felt as if someone had pulled the turf from beneath her. She opened her mouth, but she had no idea what to say.

Brian stepped forward and gently draped an arm over her shoulder. "Trust me, Kim. It's better for him to go ahead and get this out of his system. When he comes back, he'll be ready to settle down."

She frowned and nodded. "Yeah, I guess you're right. Do you know when he's going?"

Movement captured her attention, so she looked up to see David striding toward them, a quick grin followed by a look of compassion for Brian. "Sorry, buddy, tough break."

Brian slowly removed his arm from Kim's shoulder and gently nudged her toward David. "Like I told Kim—it's better Leila does this now than decide she's not ready later."

"Maybe she just has cold feet." David offered a sympathetic

grin. "I bet she comes around, and you'll be off on your honeymoon in a day or two."

"We'll see." Brian stepped away from them and waved. "I'd better go talk to some folks and thank them for coming to the party that didn't happen."

Kim and David watched Brian until he disappeared into the crowd; then David casually placed his hand in the small of Kim's back. "I wouldn't wanna be Brian now." He gave her a squeeze. "But he seems to be handling it well."

She pulled away and studied David's profile—handsome in every way, from his deep-set eyes to his strong chin. "What choice does he have?"

"Huh?"

"You said he was handling it well. What else would a guy in his place do?" Kim paused and gave him a moment to think before adding, "What would you do if I stood you up at the altar?"

He gave her a mock look of shock. "That's not something I'll ever have to worry about, is it?"

Kim shook her head. "No, of course not."

David turned her to face him and placed a hand on each of her shoulders. "That's my girl."

"Now there's something I'd like to know, David."

"What's that?" He dropped his hands to his sides and lifted one eyebrow with one of his heart-melting gazes. She had to look away to say what she needed to say.

"When were you planning to tell me about being accepted for this overseas mission?" She frowned. "I thought you were just in the discussion stage with your commanding officer."

David closed his eyes and swallowed hard. Kim folded her arms and tilted her head as she watched him try to figure out how to explain. Why didn't he just come out with it?

"I was going to tell you today." His voice was barely audible.

"Okay." She cleared her throat. "Now that I know, let's talk about it."

He gave her an apologetic look and shrugged. "What's there to talk about? I'm going over to the Middle East on a special mission."

"How long will you be gone?"

"I don't know—a couple of months, maybe a little longer?" He forced a smile, cupped her chin, and tilted her face up to his. "Not too long, though."

"What about our wedding? Will we be able to get married sometime this year?" She wasn't able to keep the sarcasm from her voice.

Suddenly his smile faded. "I was hoping to, but now I'm not sure."

"So what am I supposed to do? Send out invitations telling people that we're getting married sometime, like after you get back from your special mission, and they're invited, but we're not sure when. . ." Her voice trailed off as she started shaking.

"I'm sorry, Kim."

"If you're sorry, why did you request this assignment?" Her voice cracked, but at this point she didn't care how she sounded. David had made a monumental decision without consulting her first. Was this how it would always be?

"It's important to me. I want to be part of this mission."

"More than you want to be with me?"

"Don't be like that, Kim. You've always known how I felt about our country and my responsibility. They need me."

"I love our country, too, David, but it's not just that." She pondered the right way to put her feelings to prevent sounding selfish. "One of the things I love about you is your patriotism and commitment to protect our country. But when you asked me to marry you, I thought you wanted me to be your partner. You should have discussed it with me before you volunteered to go." Kim fought hard to control the way she sounded, but the words sounded shrill. She cleared her throat.

He narrowed his eyes, but his voice was soft. "And what would you have wanted me to do?"

"I—" She cut herself off before she said anything she might later regret. "I don't know."

David leaned toward her and reached for her hands. "Kimberly, you know how I feel about you."

"I do?"

"You should." He paused, gently ran his hand up her arm, and smiled down at her. "I love you very much. I never would have asked you to marry me if I didn't."

"But—" She stopped when he put his fingers to her lips to shush her.

"All the love in the world can't negate the fact that our country needs me. I want to do everything in my power to make this world a better place for us." He managed a half smile as he gestured across the lawn. "And for everyone here."

No way could she refute any of that, or she'd come across sounding selfish. "I guess you're right."

"I know I'm right. Now let's go see how the jilted groom is doing. We don't want to leave him alone too long, or he might think no one cares."

Kim could relate to the jilted feeling, but she still didn't say anything. As strong as she was, she knew that once she got started talking about all the reasons she was upset and hurt, she might not be able to stop. David took her by the hand and led her to Brian, who stood in the middle of a group of guys, all of them silent and looking very uncomfortable.

Kim's parents had just spoken to Brian, and they approached her as David joined Brian. "This is terrible," her mother whispered. "But at least this happened now rather than later."

With a sigh, Kim nodded. "I'm shocked, but he seems to be doing okay."

Her dad squirmed, so her mother gave her a quick hug. "I don't think your dad wants to stick around, so I'll talk to you later. We'll pray for Brian."

"I'm sure he'll appreciate it," Kim said. She strode toward David and the group that now surrounded Brian.

"Hey, buddy," David said. "Things will look better tomorrow."

One of the other men coughed, and a couple of them walked away. Kim felt even worse for Brian now.

"Do you want us to hang around?" David continued. "I don't want to leave you alone if you need us."

"Um. . ." Brian glanced around Kim then looked David in the eye. "Nah, I don't think so. I'll be fine."

"C'mon, buddy, we can do something to get your mind off things," David urged.

Kim wanted to smack him, but she just tugged him away instead. "He's not in the mood, David." She offered Brian a sympathetic look.

Brian smiled back at her then turned to David. "You're a fortunate man to have someone like Kim. You'd better hang on to her."

David possessively wrapped his arms around Kim and squeezed. "She's not going anywhere." Then he let go and pretend-punched Brian. "Hey, thanks a lot for spilling the beans about my overseas tour."

"David. . ." Kim glared at him.

Brian shot David a serious look. "I assumed you told her before you mentioned it to the rest of us. After all, she *is* your fiancée."

"Oh well, no harm done." David loosened his tie and undid the top button of his shirt. "I think I'm gonna head home and get out of this monkey suit. Wanna do something later?"

"I think I'll pass," Brian replied as he stepped back and turned. "Why don't you spend some time with Kim before you have to leave?"

Kim dropped her hands into her coat pocket. It was a cool, early spring afternoon, but as the sun headed closer to the horizon, the temperature was heading closer to freezing. She shivered.

"Cold?" David asked.

She nodded. "Yeah."

"C'mon, I'll take you home. We can go out later if you want to. I think we have more talking to do."

ها

Brian watched his best friend escort the sweetest girl in Charleston, West Virginia, toward the parking lot. David had no idea how blessed he was to have the love of a woman who'd never even think to do what Leila did.

Once upon a time, Brian had been in love with Kimberly Shaw. They'd been friends for as long as he could remember—since sometime in early elementary school. She was athletic, so they played on the same county-run soccer team. By the time they reached middle school, she'd moved on to the girl's volleyball team at school, while he went out for football. Kim remained his friend, but things had changed. Boys liked her, and she trusted Brian enough to confide her deepest thoughts and feelings. Somewhere along the way, he'd fallen in love with her, and it hit him hard when one of his buddies gave her his class ring in high school. Brian wished he'd made his move before it was too late, but he didn't want to risk losing what he had with Kim.

He managed to stand on the sidelines of her life until his friend dumped her right before their big senior event at school. When Kim called crying, he offered to be her date, and she'd accepted. Too bad he'd wimped out on letting her know then how he felt—but he wasn't willing to risk scaring her away. Instead, he encouraged her to try new things and not let any guy get the best of her. He figured if they were meant to be together, it would happen one of these days. Surely God would see to that, right? He prayed every night for some opening into the romantic side of Kim's heart.

When he'd met David during a National Guard weekend, he'd been happy to meet someone else from his hometown. David had grown up on the other side of Charleston, so he'd gone to a different school. Brian invited him to church, and David agreed without a moment's hesitation.

Kim didn't seem all that interested in David at first. However, when David set his mind to pursuing her, she didn't stand a chance. That was two years ago, and now they were engaged.

Brian wanted to kick himself in the backside. What a chump he'd been. Meeting Leila had given him a little ray of sunshine. She was beauty-pageant pretty. Leila was a talented musician and singer, who loved doing solos in church. She laughed at his jokes and made him feel as if he were the only other person in the room. She still didn't match up to Kim, yet he was able to convince himself that he was in love with her. And since he couldn't have Kim, he knew he could grow old with Leila and never want to be with anyone else. She'd talked him into not reenlisting with the Guard because she didn't like him going away so often. He was willing to do whatever it took to make a marriage work.

God, why did this have to happen? Now what?

&

The second Kim closed the door behind her, she leaned against it and tilted her head upward. *Lord, what do You want me to do? I'm angry at David, and I don't know if I'll ever understand why it's so important to leave—especially now that we're supposed to be planning our life together.*

Guilt flooded her as she straightened and plodded toward her bedroom to change into her jeans. David said he'd be back in a couple of hours, so she had time to straighten up a bit and get herself mentally and emotionally ready for their talk. However, as the minutes ticked away, she felt even worse than when he'd dropped her off.

When the doorbell rang, Kimberly steeled herself and flung open the door. David handed her a grocery store bouquet.

"I'll put these in some water, and we can go."

Once she finished arranging the flowers, she turned to David, who quirked an eyebrow and grinned. "You okay?"

Kim shrugged. "I guess."

He touched her arm and broadened his smile. "I won't be gone long. You know how quickly the months fly by."

"That's not the point, David, and you know it." She had to speak her mind. "I'm not as upset about you leaving as I am the fact that you never discussed it with me."

"Do I have to discuss everything with you?"

"Not everything," she replied. "Just the important stuff. The stuff that impacts us."

"Kim, I love you, and I thought I knew you well enough to trust that you'd understand." He pulled her into his arms and rested his chin on her head as her mind swirled. When he drew back and looked into her eyes, she saw that familiar spark. "I'm just glad you're nothing like Leila. You're a good woman who'll be there for me, no matter what."

two

Kimberly's heart ached as she thought about the meaning of "no matter what." If it involved David's making decisions without consulting her, she wasn't so sure she could live up to his expectations.

David shook his head. "Being a military wife can be rough, but it has its rewards, too."

She stood there for a moment as her thoughts scrambled in her head. "I'm sure." Her voice caught in her throat.

"Why don't you get to know some other military wives and girlfriends and hang out with them?" he said. "It'll make the time go by faster."

"I might do that."

"You do still want to marry me, don't you, Kimberly?" He twirled a lock of her hair then tucked it behind her ear.

Kim swallowed hard as she frowned up at him. "Yes, of course I do, but I wonder. . ." In spite of trying to settle her shaky nerves, she couldn't keep the accusatory tone from her voice. "I just wonder if you want the military more than you want to marry me."

"Don't tell me what I really want," he said softly, "because I know. I want you."

"But you want the military even more."

David blinked and half smiled. "The military is a bigger calling for me, yes." He gently rested his hands on her shoulders and looked down at her until she allowed herself to meet his gaze. "But that doesn't negate my feelings for you in the least, Kimberly. You know how I feel about you. That hasn't changed one iota." He hesitated before adding, "My acceptance of this mission wasn't done without quite a bit of prayer. I feel that this is what God wants me to do."

How could she respond to that? They stood in silence for several minutes before Kim finally shook her head. "I don't want to change anything right now. If you've been called to this mission, then go. I'll wait for you." She cast her glance downward and pulled her bottom lip between her teeth to keep her chin from quivering.

He tilted her face toward his. "Are you sure?"

Sort of. She nodded.

"I'll talk to Brian and get him to look after you."

Kim bristled. "I don't need anyone to look after me. I'm perfectly capable of taking care of myself."

David leaned back and laughed. "Now there's the girl I fell in love with. Independent and strong."

"But I don't mind looking after him. After all, he just got jilted."

"Yes," David agreed. "That's an excellent idea. Do you want me to talk to him first?"

"I don't think that'll be necessary," Kim said. "Remember, I've known him practically all my life. And he introduced us."

"True. Maybe you can return the favor and find someone to help get his mind off Leila."

"It's not that easy," she said. "But I'm a good listener, so if he needs to talk, I'll just be there for him."

"Maybe some nice Christian girl will come into the salon, and you can talk him up."

Kim couldn't help but laugh. "Yeah, I'll hold her captive with a can of hair spray and some scissors."

"Attagirl." David chucked her under the chin. "Then you can give her a gorgeous haircut that he won't be able to resist. Whatever works to bring him back to life."

≈

As difficult as it had been to hear that David was leaving, after he'd boarded the bus, Kim wasn't as devastated as she thought she'd be. When she turned around, she saw Brian standing by her car, watching. . .waiting. He grinned and motioned for her to join him.

"What are you doing here?" Kim shielded her eyes from the sun.

"David told me when he was leaving. I asked if it was okay for me to be here for you, and he thought that was a great idea."

They stood and watched as the bus took off down the street. After it was out of sight, Brian patted her on the shoulder. "I sure hope everything turns out like you want it to, Kim. You certainly deserve the best."

"Thanks." She smiled up at him. "I just wish he'd talked to me about it earlier."

"He really should have. I told him that when he first decided to request this assignment."

Her head snapped around. "You did? Why didn't *you* tell me then?"

"I wanted to, but David reminded me that it wasn't my place. He said he wanted to tell you, and I agreed that would be best." Brian shifted his weight and turned to face her. "But if I'd known then what I know now, I would have given him an ultimatum that if he didn't tell you right away, I would have."

"That's what hurts."

He gave her a brotherly hug. "Need some company for the day?"

"Not really. I have a pile of laundry and some hairstyle books I wanted to read."

"Let me know if you need me." After she unlocked her car, he held the door. "The least you can let me do is pick you up for church on Sunday—for old times' sake. I'm sure David wouldn't mind."

David's words about looking after Brian rang through her head. "Of course he wouldn't. He knows we're like brother and sister. Sounds good." She got in her car and took off, only casting one quick glance in the rearview mirror to see Brian standing there, still watching.

Carrie called shortly after she got home. "I got it!"

"Huh?" Kim knew whatever it was had to be good by the sound of Carrie's squeal of excitement. "What did you get?"

"You know, that job in Chicago."

Kim racked her brain, trying to remember something about Carrie applying for a job in Chicago, but nothing came to her. "I'm sorry, Carrie. I don't know where my mind has been, but I don't have a clue what you're talking about."

"That's probably because I didn't tell you where it was. All I said was that I was being considered for a promotion."

"Oh yeah. You got it?" Kim had assumed it was in Charleston. "So you have to move to Chicago?"

"Just temporarily," Carrie replied. "I'll train there and eventually come back here to manage the West Virginia district."

That was a relief. "At least you'll be back. When do you leave?"

"Tomorrow."

ða

Brian recovered from the public jilting much more quickly than he thought he would. What bothered him more than the wedding falling through was the humiliation of everyone staring at him when he found out Leila wasn't showing up. If it hadn't been for Kim, he would have been too embarrassed to show his face in church—at least for a while.

He'd taken his time getting ready. Kim had wanted to go to the early service, and he suspected it was for him, since they wouldn't see all the usual people.

The instant she opened the door, he gave her a once-over. "Hey, you look pretty good for a lonely woman."

She flicked her scarf at him. "Stop it, Brian. You don't have to go there with me."

"I'm serious. I half expected to see red-rimmed eyes and that drab brown dress you used to wear when you didn't feel good."

Kim pointed to her eyes. "If you look behind the concealer, you'll see the red. As for the dress, I sent it to Goodwill last year when David told me it was the ugliest thing he'd ever seen and I looked absolutely hideous in it."

A burst of anger rose in Brian's chest. "He told you that?" Kim couldn't look hideous if she tried.

She bobbed her head. "It's not like you don't agree. In fact, everyone I know hated that dress."

"The dress wasn't attractive, but you were still pretty."

"Oh, you." She pulled out her keys and lightly pushed him toward the door. "Let's drop the fake stuff. We've known each other too long to be dishing out anything that's not real."

He knew how she hated compliments. She'd always been that way—even when their senior class voted her cutest girl. In fact, she'd reminded him that puppies were cute, so she could win the award for looking like a dog.

❧

For the next three weeks, Kim and Brian went to church together, but that was it. The only other thing she knew he did was work—totally not like Brian who loved nothing more than to be right in the middle of the social action.

Finally, she couldn't stand it anymore, and she remembered David urging her to help keep Brian's mind off Leila, so on Tuesday she went to the back room at the Snappy Scissors and called him during her lunch break.

"Hey, Kim. Something wrong?"

"No. . .well, maybe. What's up with you? Where do you hide all week?"

He didn't answer right away, but Kim could hear him breathing.

"So you're giving me the silent treatment? You acted perfectly fine on Sunday."

"I've been working." His voice sounded off. She'd known Brian long enough to realize something was up—and he wasn't going to talk without some not-so-gentle prodding from her.

"What're you doing after work tonight?"

"I'm behind on paperwork," he replied. "Look, Kim, I'm

really busy right now."

"No, you look, Brian. I've had one man keep secrets then take off for the other side of the world. I'm not letting one of my best friends do this to me. Either tell me what's going on, or I'm coming over tonight, whether you like it or not."

After a brief pause, he said, "Okay, but not tonight. Why don't you and I meet somewhere for lunch tomorrow?"

"That's fine. How about we meet at the Blossom Deli at eleven thirty tomorrow?"

"Great. I'll treat you to a Reuben."

"Be still, my heart," she said with a swoon. "You certainly know the way to get my mind off my sorrows."

"Yeah, yeah," he said, his tone lightening up a touch. "You say that to all the guys."

"Right," she replied. "I want to warn you, though. I need to vent."

"You and me both." He chuckled. "Just make sure you don't stand me up. My fragile ego can't handle that again."

Kim heard between the lines, and she knew there was seriousness behind his playful tone. "You've always been able to trust me, Brian. When have I ever let you down?"

"Never. You're not that kind of girl. See you tomorrow. I need to get back to these invoices, or I might not be able to pay for lunch tomorrow."

"It's my turn to treat anyway," Kim said, "so don't worry about it."

After they hung up, she stayed in the break room, got her salad out of the fridge, and sat down at the table in the corner. Tuesdays were typically slow, so only three stylists were scheduled, and they staggered their lunch breaks. She was relieved to be alone with her thoughts.

*

All afternoon Brian struggled to keep his thoughts on business. Kimberly Shaw's image kept popping into his head.

"Knock, knock."

Brian glanced up to see Jack Morrow smiling at him from

the door. "Just wanted to tell you what a good job you did on the quarterly financials. Patterson was impressed."

"For a CEO of the largest tool distributor in the world, it doesn't take much to impress him, does it?"

"C'mon, Brian. You're the best comptroller we've ever had. Everyone thinks so."

Brian took his hand off the computer mouse and settled back in his chair. "Whaddya need, Jack?"

"Who says I need anything?" The district manager took a couple of steps into Brian's office and closed the door behind him. "Mind if I come in?"

Brian laughed. "Of course not." He gestured to the chair across from his desk. "Have a seat and tell me what's on your mind."

Jack glanced around the office, obviously stalling for time. Finally, he looked Brian in the eye. "Anything I can do?"

"Do about what? What are you talking about?" Brian asked.

"You know. Leila. I'm a good listener."

"I appreciate that, but I'm fine." Brian smiled. "She actually did me a favor."

"Then what's been on your mind the past few weeks?"

"Why?"

"I don't know. . ." Jack glanced down at his hands as he steepled his fingers and studied them before looking Brian in the eye. "You've done a great job here, but you haven't been your old self since the wedding. I'm concerned."

"I'm just fine. Leila and I would have made things work, but I don't think we were all that great of a match."

Jack stood up and flashed a sympathetic smile. "Good. I just wanted you to know that you can talk to me."

"Thanks, Jack. I appreciate it."

"See ya."

After Jack left, Brian closed his eyes. *Lord, give me the strength to get past all this. I appreciate the concern of my friends, but it's time to move on.*

The rest of the afternoon went by in a blur as he finished another report and started a new one. Brian was thankful to have such a mentally consuming job. Although his co-workers probably assumed he was immersing himself in his work because of Leila, he knew he was trying to get past thoughts of what could have been between him and Kimberly.

⁂

The second Kim spotted Brian rounding the corner toward Blossom's, her pulse quickened, and some old feelings flooded her, bringing her back to much younger days when she'd fantasized about Brian telling her he cared more about her than he was letting on. The one time she thought they might get romantic, he'd gotten all flustered and challenged her to a race, which she knew he did to change the mood. That was probably for the best.

"You look great, Kimberly." Brian hugged her and gave her a kiss on the cheek before turning toward the door of the deli.

Kim fought hard to keep her nerves intact. She chattered incessantly about work and everything else she could think of. When there was a lull between them, she told herself the only reason she felt this way was that David was gone. Brian was like a brother to her—nothing else. And that was all it could ever be.

"Have you thought about going back to the singles group?" Brian asked.

She held up her hand and pointed to the diamond. "No, how about you?"

"Yeah, but it seems weird. Wanna go sometime?" He cleared his throat and quickly added, "Just until David comes back. I just thought maybe it would be fun to see some old friends."

Kim smiled. She was glad Brian let her know what she needed from her. "Of course I'll go with you, Brian. You should get back in circulation. You're too good of a catch to be roaming around without a good woman." She almost choked on those words.

A strange expression flickered across his face, but he quickly recovered. He laughed. "Now that's a new one."

"It's true," she insisted. "I can't imagine why any girl would ever let you go. You're sweet, smart, and fun—not to mention a great-looking guy who loves Jesus."

Color crept up his cheeks as he shook his head and made a face. "Apparently, that's not enough for some women."

"I think Leila will look back at what she did and regret it, but you'll be taken by then, I'm sure."

Brian shifted in his seat before reaching across the table for her hand. "Thank you, Kim. Now let's discuss the singles group. Wanna start tonight?"

If it weren't for David encouraging her to do whatever it took to get Brian's mind off Leila, she wouldn't have considered it. She slowly nodded. "Okay."

"Why don't I pick you up at six?"

"Want me to fix supper?"

"Maybe next week. Tonight's my treat. It's my turn, remember?"

She smiled and nodded. "You're on," she said as she wrapped what was left of her sandwich. "I need to get back to work."

Kim's schedule was booked the rest of the afternoon, so she didn't have time to ponder her situation. When closing time came, she hung up her apron and got her station ready for the next day. As she wiped down the counter and prepared her combs and brushes, the owner of the salon kept up a constant stream of chatter.

"I'm whipped," Jasmine said. "I can't wait to go home, take a shower, and curl up in front of the TV. What're you doing tonight?"

"Singles group at church," Kim replied.

Jasmine stopped midsweep. "Singles group? Do I sense trouble in paradise? What's up with you and David?"

"Nothing. I'm going with Brian so he doesn't have to face everyone alone."

"Oh," Jasmine said, nodding her understanding. "That poor boy getting stood up like that—and in front of all his family and friends. I bet he's a wreck."

"No, actually, he's handling it quite well."

Jasmine tilted her head and regarded Kim for a moment. "Ya know, if it weren't for David being in the picture, I think you and Brian would make a cute couple."

Kim let out a nervous laugh. "I don't think so. We're more like brother and sister. We've known each other since I can remember."

"And you're very close. Good friends for life, right?"

"That's right," Kim agreed.

"Well, I think it's important for married couples to be friends. The chemistry between them will come and go, but friendship lasts forever."

She should know, Kim thought; *Jasmine's been married almost thirty years.*

"Were you and Wayne friends before you got married?"

Jasmine grinned. "Yep. His family lived right next door to mine growing up."

"I never knew that. Why didn't you tell me?"

"You never asked." Jasmine reached for the dustpan and finished sweeping. "But that's a moot point, right? You're just keeping Brian company until he meets someone else."

"That's right." Kim pulled her bottom lip between her teeth as she thought about Brian meeting someone new.

"Okay, looks like I'm all done here," Jasmine said as she brushed her hands together. "I hope Wayne has dinner ready for me when I get home, 'cuz I'm too tired to cook."

"See you tomorrow."

Kim finished her work then headed home to get ready for the singles group. She'd barely had time to shower and change into some khakis and a sweater when the doorbell rang.

"Hey," she said as she flung open the door.

"Hey, yourself," Brian replied. "I'm starving. Ready to go?"

After dinner at the same diner they'd been frequenting since childhood, they rode to the church in silence. Brian was the only person Kim was this comfortable not talking with, and she knew he felt the same way.

As the Bible study progressed, Kim enjoyed the camaraderie among old friends and a few new people she'd just met. After she and David got engaged, they joined a couples group. The time flew, so when they said their closing prayer, she was sad.

"We need a show of hands to see who all's going bowling Friday night," the group leader said.

Brian nudged her. "Wanna go?"

"I don't know if that's such a good idea with David being gone."

"Come on. David doesn't expect you to sit home every night while he's gone. At least you'll be with a group."

She hesitated. "It just seems strange."

"Strange?" Brian asked with a teasing tone. "This is me, Brian, you're talking to."

"Yeah, I know, but. . ."

"Okay, if you're that uncomfortable about it, I understand. But I think it'll be good for me to go." Brian lifted his hand, and the leader nodded his acknowledgment.

Kim really enjoyed bowling, and it had been a while. "Okay, I might as well join you," she said as she followed suit and raised her hand.

"Thanks for doing this, Kim."

"What's a friend for?"

The smile that spread over Brian's face warmed her all over. She wondered if he realized she was doing this as much for herself as for him.

three

On Friday night, Brian melted at the thought of hanging out with Kim. They must have bowled together at least a dozen times in their lives, but it never felt like this—almost like a date. He had to force himself to remember David. They drove to the bowling alley together.

Each time she stepped up to the line and got into position, he couldn't take his eyes off her. Everything about Kimberly Shaw put his senses into high gear.

She glanced over her shoulder and grinned. "What are you staring at, Brian?"

"You."

"I don't want you watching me when I do this."

He blinked then forced a laugh. "Why? Need some lessons?"

"From you?" she said as she wriggled her eyebrows. "Not in this lifetime. However, if you need help from me, I'll be there."

Suddenly he felt as though someone had pulled the plug on his life raft. She'd pretty much summed up what was between them. He needed way more help than she did.

Kim continued standing at the line. "We don't have all day," Matthew Hayes said. "C'mon, Kim, just roll it."

"I'm just getting into position—trying to find my groove. You want me to knock down some pins, don't you?" she asked as she shifted from side to side.

"Yeah, but it needs to happen sometime tonight."

She cut another sarcastic glance over at Matthew then turned back around to face the pins. "Brian," she said softly, "I need you."

Brian looked down at the floor to keep from showing the impact her simple comment had on him. When he heard

27

Kim's soft voice calling his name, he almost thought he was hearing things.

"Brian, the lady needs you," Matthew said. "Go help her so we can get through this game."

"Uh. . .sure." Brian hopped up and joined Kim.

"I sort of forgot which foot to step out on." Kim glanced at him apologetically. "Sorry. It's been a long time."

If Brian could have captured that moment and held it in his pocket, he would have. "Remember, you like to walk down in four steps. Since you're left-handed, you'll start out on your left foot so you wind up on the right foot. As you approach, you swing back to get momentum. Then when you take your fourth step, you swing the ball forward and release." He gave her shoulders a squeeze and quickly let go.

Kim closed her eyes, mouthed what he'd just said, then opened her eyes and nodded. "Okay, I think I've got it. Thanks." She took a step but stopped.

"Ki—im," Matthew said. "Just roll the ball."

"Want me to talk you through it again?" Brian asked softly.

"If you don't mind." She didn't look up, but Brian felt connected to Kim—almost as though they were a couple. And he liked it—way too much.

"Okay, pull back and slowly go, left. . .right. . .left. . .right and release."

❧

Kim held her breath as she watched her ball slowly roll toward the pins. She'd let go a little too far to the left, but as the ball made its way closer to the pins, it started to veer toward the center. She did a little shuffle with her feet and scooted to the right.

"Looks like a good one, Kim!" Matthew hollered.

The ball came in between the front pin and the one just to the left and behind it. A couple of pins fell, and the remaining ones wobbled, until every last one of them fell. The ball clunked into the back, and there wasn't a single pin standing!

Kim jumped up and down, clapping. Brian came toward

her with his arms open wide. She didn't hesitate a second before rushing toward him and giving him a huge hug. He lifted her off the floor then gently set her back down. When she glanced up into his eyes, she saw something different.

And her insides did a flippy thing—just like what had happened the first time she thought she might be in love with him. Her heart hammered as she put more distance between them. The feeling surprised her.

"If I didn't know the two of you were just buddies, I'd be worried for David," Brenda called out from a couple of lanes away.

Kim quickly glanced away as her cheeks flamed. When she recovered and opened her mouth to thank Brian for his coaching, her voice got stuck in her throat, and nothing came out. He grinned and winked, so she nodded and smiled right back at him, thankful he couldn't read her mind.

"Good job, Kim!" Matthew said as he cast a look of annoyance toward Brenda. Then he turned back and smiled at Kim. "Just don't take so long next time, okay?"

"She just bowled a strike," Brian said in her defense. "She doesn't even have to roll a second ball."

Kim looked back and forth between Brian and Matthew, who'd lifted his eyebrows. Brian slowly nodded.

"True," Matthew said. "You're up now, Brian."

"Need any help?" Kim asked Brian as he selected his ball from the return. She had to work hard at controlling the shakiness in her voice, but she needed to act as natural as possible. "I'm pretty good at this, ya know."

"Yeah, got any pointers?" Brian asked.

"Just roll the ball and keep it out of the gutter. If everything works out right, you'll knock 'em all down, and you won't have to roll a second ball."

Brian chuckled. "Excellent advice from a pro. I'll see if I can manage that."

Kim really wanted him to make a strike. The last time she'd bowled had been with David, who loved the fact that his score was more than double hers. That was almost a year ago, but she remembered how he'd actually laughed when her ball rolled into the gutter.

Brian's ball hit the front pin head-on, and the two back corner pins were still standing. He turned around to face her with a lopsided grin. "I guess I just don't have your touch."

"I guess not," she said.

After his ball returned, he rolled it down and managed to knock over one of the remaining pins. He sat down next to Kim and patted her on the back. "Looks like you might carry the team tonight, Miss Kim."

"Okay, you two," Matthew said as he stood to take his turn. "Let me show you how it's done."

He left three pins standing. "Want me to give you a few tips?" Kim asked.

Matthew rolled his eyes. "Brian, my friend, I think you've created a monster." Then he gestured for Kim to join him. "Sure. Come on up and tell me how to pick these up."

Kim stood next to him and studied the pins before she gestured. "What you want to do is aim for the spot between those two on the right; then if you hit them at the right angle, one of them will swing over to the left and knock the other one down."

She noticed Matthew and Brian exchanging an amused glance, but it was all in fun. As Matthew took his approach toward the foul line, he swung and released the ball. It rode the edge for about ten feet then swung over and smacked the two pins on the right at exactly the angle needed to knock the other pin down. He made a spare!

Once again, Kim jumped up and shoved her fist into the air. "See? I told you! All you have to do is listen to me."

"Yeah," Matthew said as he headed for his seat. "I gotta give you credit. You knew exactly what I needed to do." He pointed to Brian. "Now you need to give him a little more coaching, and we just might win this game."

At the end of the night, Brian actually had the highest

score on the team, Matthew came in second, Matthew's girlfriend, Ashley, was third, and Kim came up last with a score that barely broke one hundred. "I don't know how that happened," she told Brian as they left the bowling alley and walked toward his car. "I got off to such a good start."

"It was just a bad night," Brian said. "We should probably come back and practice before we bowl with everyone else."

"Yeah. I feel pretty uncoordinated after tonight," she said. "But it was fun."

Brian held the door until she got in; then he ran around to his side to join her. "I had fun, too."

Kim's heart lightened. "I'm glad you're doing so well after what Leila did. I'm still in shock about it."

"Yes, but it turned out okay. She called me yesterday."

"She did? What did she say?"

Brian put the key into the ignition before turning to face Kim. "She said she knew the night before the wedding, but she thought it was just nerves at first."

Kim remembered Leila stuffing herself with food. "That's no excuse."

"I know, but don't be too hard on her, Kim. Leila's never been sure of herself."

Kim wanted to tell Brian that everyone had moments of not being confident or sure, but that was still no excuse to do what Leila had done. However, he was obviously too much of a gentleman to say anything bad about his ex.

"So what now?" Kim asked.

Brian shrugged. "Who knows?"

"Do you think she'll change her mind and decide she wants to marry you?"

"No, that's not gonna happen," he replied. "After being stood up at the altar and realizing I was okay with it, I knew it wasn't meant to be."

Kim felt an immediate sense of relief. "You're an amazing guy, Brian."

He winked at her. "I wonder if David realizes how fortunate

he is to have a woman like you."

She shrugged. "I'm the fortunate one." Her stomach churned, and she couldn't look Brian in the eye.

Brian pulled up to Kim's house and waited until she walked up the sidewalk, opened the door, and waved. On her way back to the bedroom, she dropped her handbag and jacket on the back of the sofa. After changing into her pajamas, she booted up her computer and pounded out an e-mail to David, letting him know what all was going on at home. Maybe sharing her experiences with him through e-mail would help her feel better. She was disappointed that he hadn't answered her last e-mail, but he'd told her it wasn't always easy getting on the Internet from where he was.

20

Of all times for this to happen, Brian couldn't figure out why he couldn't get his feelings in check for Kim. She'd been his best friend since forever ago. In the past when this happened, he'd been able to refocus and get things back to how they should be.

Lord, I want to do Your will. Please give me the strength to get through whatever feelings I have for Kimberly. I want to be there for her since David's gone, so staying away from her isn't an option.

He opened his eyes and swallowed hard before bowing his head again. *I guess it is an option if that's the direction You want me to go. Just make it obvious, because I've never been good at reading between the lines.*

Brian thought about all the little nuances of his relationship with Kim. When they were little, they played sports together and exchanged baseball cards. In middle school they vacillated between being best friends and arguing over small, insignificant things, like whether to ride bikes or hang out and listen to music. As he looked back, he knew he'd picked arguments when he wasn't sure how to handle his attraction to her. Throughout high school they went to each other for advice about relationships—always regarding other people, because they never discussed their feelings for each other. And since they'd been such good friends, he'd never wanted to make her uncomfortable by trying to change their relationship.

After trying to read but not being able to focus on the words, Brian powered up his computer and checked his e-mail. No word from David yet, but that didn't surprise him. David had said his Internet access would be sporadic.

Finally, after answering all his e-mail and clicking on a few links from friends, Brian felt sleepy enough to go to bed. He said one last prayer for guidance before closing his eyes and falling asleep.

❧

"You look more chipper today," Jasmine said the second Kim walked through the door on Monday morning. "How was bowling?"

"I lost, but I had a great time."

Jasmine grinned. "That's what really matters." She turned and picked up a magazine from the counter and handed it to Kim. "I brought you a bridal magazine."

"Thanks." Kim took it, flipped through the pages for a few seconds, then slipped it into her tote. "I'll look at it later."

Kim went to her station and got ready for her first client before turning back to the other hairdresser. "Ya know, Brian is such a good guy. I can't imagine why Leila would do what she did."

"Like I said before, I can't imagine why you and Brian aren't together," Jasmine retorted.

Kim froze in place for a second before she cleared her throat. "That would be a disaster. We've been friends forever, and we know way too much about each other to make it work."

"Why?" Jasmine turned and faced her. "It seems to me that knowing a lot about someone and still caring about him is a good thing."

Kim lifted a shoulder, paused, then let it drop. "It really

doesn't matter now anyway. I'm engaged to David."

Jasmine contorted her mouth and nodded. "True. I just hope y'all don't turn into one of those perpetually engaged couples who can't set the date."

"Oh, that won't happen. As soon as he gets back from. . . well, from wherever he is in the Middle East, we'll pick the day."

"I hope so for your sake," Jasmine said as her attention was diverted to the person who'd just walked in the door. "Your client's here."

The rest of the day was busy, which was exactly what Kim needed. As soon as the shop closed, she quickly cleaned her station and went home. She pulled the bridal magazine out of her bag and started looking at the pictures. But nothing about it interested her, so she tossed it on the end table and went to check her e-mail. When she spotted David's name in the incoming mail, she grinned.

To: KShaw
From: DJenner
Subject: Re: Missing you

Hey there, hon! Sorry so much time lapses between my e-mails, but our Internet connection is very sketchy. Seems like it's down as much as it's up. I'm glad you have Brian there to keep you company (and busy—) while I'm out of the country. I hope we can complete our mission soon, but it's not looking good at the moment. The insurgent activity is at an all-time high, and it's very dangerous here. Wish I could tell you more, but this mission has to remain top secret to protect everyone involved.

Tell Brian thanks for watching after my favorite girl. Sounds like you had a great time at the bowling alley. Mostly I'm glad you're not sitting home being lonely. It makes my job easier if I don't have to worry about you. And I'm sure you've been good at helping keep Brian's mind off being left at the altar. My mission is here, and yours is with Brian.

Can't wait to read your next e-mail. While you're back in the States having fun, have a little extra fun for me.

Love you, babe!
David

Kim read David's message over several times before she finally clicked out of it and sank back in her chair. It was wonderful to hear from him. So what was up with the hollow feeling?

She instinctively reached for the phone to call Brian, but she quickly pulled back. Yeah, he'd understand and sympathize, but she needed to stop leaning on him so much.

The sudden ringing of the phone startled her. When she picked it up and heard Brian's voice, she laughed.

"What's so funny?" he asked.

"I was just thinking about calling you. What's up?"

"When I got home, there was a message on the phone from Matthew about the whitewater rafting trip on the New River Saturday, and I wondered if you wanted to go."

Kim started to say no, but she thought about David's e-mail and how he'd encouraged her to help keep Brian's mind off Leila. Besides, it would be fun, and it would give her something else to write David about. It was harmless, and they'd be so active she wouldn't have time to think about how Brian was starting to make her feel. "Sure, I'd like that."

"You don't sound all that enthusiastic."

"Sorry. I just got home and read an e-mail from David."

She heard a quick intake of air on the other end of the line before Brian cleared his throat. "So what's he up to?"

"I wish I knew. He just said something about how dangerous it was there—"

Brian interrupted. "Enough to worry you, right?"

"Yeah. He also said to thank you for watching out for me."

Brian chuckled. "You watching out for me is more like it."

"Right. So if I go rafting, what all do I need to bring?"

"Food," he replied. "Lots of it."

"With you along, that goes without saying. Anything else?"

"Nah, I think we're good."

♦

Matthew assigned people to rafts then gestured toward the park employee who took the cue to give explicit instructions on safety. "We haven't lost anyone before, and we don't want to start now. Keep your eye on your buddy and don't take off your life jacket, no matter how good of a swimmer you are."

Matthew nodded toward the water. "Let's go have us some fun!"

Groups of four positioned themselves in the rafts. Brian held Kim's hand as she got in; then he followed. Minutes later their raft had been taken over by the swiftly moving water.

"Take it easy, Brian," Kim said as they bounced along the rapids. "I don't want to lose my breakfast."

Brian laughed. "You think I can do anything about this?"

"Stop leaning. I don't want to get dumped into this crazy river."

"But you look so cute wet." He grinned and made a gesture around his head. "I especially like it when your hair is all tangled and plastered." The other two people, Shawn and Ashley, laughed.

"I'm serious. Stop trying to tip the raft."

The very thought of anything happening to Kim made him shudder. "I won't lean anymore. But if you do fall overboard, I'll go in after you."

She scowled then broke into a grin. "Yeah, and we'll both drown." She paused then gave him one of her warning looks.

Brian felt like he already was drowning. And rafting on the New River had nothing to do with it.

Shawn and Ashley had a loud conversation going with the people in the raft just ahead of them. Kim glared at Brian and whispered, "Just stop trying to tip the raft, Brian. I mean it. If you don't cut it out, I'll tell everyone about the bodysurfing incident."

"You wouldn't."

"Don't test me."

෨

Kim had more fun on Saturday than she could remember having in a long time. Brian brought her home, helped her carry her bag and cooler inside, then left to get cleaned up. As soon as she was alone, she showered and slipped into a jogging suit before sitting down in front of her computer. To her disappointment, there were no e-mails from David. She started a new letter to tell him about her day.

> To: DJenner
> From: KShaw
> Subject: River fun
>
> Dear David,
>   I just got back from having more fun than I can remember.

No, that didn't come across right. Kim thought for a moment before deleting it.

> Dear David,
>   I just got back from a whitewater rafting trip on the New River. We had a lot of fun, but it would have been more fun with you there.
>   Matthew arranged the groups and made sure we knew the rules about the buddy system and life jackets. I hope he has kids someday, because he'd make a wonderful father. Matthew put us on the same raft with a new couple, Shawn and Ashley. The river was normal, but Brian made sure we had plenty of excitement. Every chance he got, he tried to tip the raft, until I told him to knock it off, or I'd tell everyone about the time he wiped out bodysurfing. Remember that? I'll never forget our church trip to the coast when you and I finally got together.
>   Anyway, after a few hair-raising experiences with Brian

trying to tip the raft, we finally made it to the end, where our food was waiting. After we ate, Brian took the rest of the food home with him. I don't think he'll starve anytime soon.

Everyone says to tell you hi. Please stay safe. I want you to come home soon.

Miss you!

Love,
Kimberly

She sat back and read the letter again before clicking SEND. Then she grabbed the bridal magazine Jasmine had given her and headed straight for bed. Brian had asked her to go to the early service the next morning, and she said she'd meet him there.

≈

Brian dabbed more lotion on the spot he'd missed with the sunscreen before the rafting trip. He compared himself to David, who never burned but only got darker in the sun. Brian couldn't help the fact that he was blond.

He slipped into his polo shirt, combed his hair, and took one last look in the mirror. He couldn't do anything about the red splotch on the side of his face but wait for the sunburn to go away. Kim had teased him and offered some concealer. He'd quipped back that he'd have to rub it all over his face for it to do any good, so no thanks. Then he changed the subject and talked about church.

Kim agreed to go to the early service, in spite of the fact that she preferred sleeping an extra hour on Sundays. She'd given Brian a hard time about his antics during the rafting trip, but she came through for him in the end. And she'd packed enough food to feed everyone on their raft and still have leftovers, which she'd sent home with him.

He pulled into the parking lot, picked his Bible up off the seat, then walked around the church toward the front steps. When he glanced up, his mouth instantly went dry. On the top step, standing next to Kim by the double doors, was Leila.

four

Kim saw the look of shock on Brian's face, and she instantly wanted to comfort him. However, she felt stymied by the fact that Leila was right there beside her.

"Hey, Kim," Brian said before turning to face his former fiancée. "Leila, you look nice. How are you today?"

Leila cleared her throat and shifted from one foot to the other. "I'm fine, Brian. Maybe we can talk later?"

Brian shrugged. "Sure, whatever." He looked back at Kim. "Are we still sitting together, or have you made other plans?"

"We're still sitting together." Kim turned to Leila, who'd just stopped to ask if she'd seen Brian. "It was nice talking to you, Leila. Maybe we can get together sometime?" She had to force softness in her voice, because there was no point in showing her animosity—especially not on the church steps.

Leila glanced down as she took a small step back. "Maybe."

"Have a good day," Kim said before turning and linking arms with Brian. "C'mon, let's go sit down."

After they sat and picked up their hymnals, Brian elbowed Kim. "Well? Are you gonna fill me in on the powwow?"

"There's nothing to say other than the fact that she wanted to know if I'd seen you."

Brian tilted his head and quirked a brow. "What did you tell her?"

Kim studied him for a moment before answering. "Why are you so concerned?"

"I just wondered, that's all. Don't forget, she and I were engaged to be married, and if things had gone as planned, I'd be sitting here with her."

"Well, too bad you're not," Kim quipped. "You're stuck with me instead."

"Yeah, too bad, huh?" he said with a lopsided grin. "I think I came out the winner here."

Kim's heart warmed. "Thanks, Brian. That was sweet."

"Don't get used to it."

"Oh, trust me, I know better than that."

The pastor approached the pulpit, so they focused their attention on the service. After the last hymn was sung, the pastor announced that the nursery was shorthanded, and they were in dire need of people to volunteer to watch the children during adult Bible study between the early and late services.

Brian lifted an eyebrow and tilted his head. "Wanna go watch some kids with me?"

She angled her head forward and looked at him from beneath hooded eyes. "You're kidding, right?"

"No, I'm not kidding. They need help, and we're able to do it."

"You know I've never been around children that much."

"They're just little people," he said.

"Yeah," she agreed. "With high-pitched voices and constant motion."

"Oh, come on, Kimberly. It'll be fun." He gave her a challenging glare. "Or are you scared? Maybe you're right. Some people can't handle the pint-size set."

Not one to back down to a challenge, she rolled her eyes. "Oh, all right. I'll do it."

Brian's mouth spread in a wide grin. "I thought you might." He patted her hand. "You'll do fine. Just watch me and do what I do."

"All righty," she said as they headed toward the church nursery. Secretly, Kim hoped others would be waiting to help out in the nursery and her services wouldn't be needed. However, just the opposite was the case. The sound of children's voices with their harried parents standing nearby, hoping to be relieved so they could attend Bible class, let her know she was a welcome sight.

"I'm so glad y'all are here," Carmen said from the split

door. "Please come in and wash your hands. I need to change this one's diaper; then we can decide who does what."

After she put a clean diaper on the child she was holding, Carmen turned toward Kim. "Any questions before I leave?"

"You're leaving?" Kim asked, her throat tight from panic.

Carmen smiled and let out a little chuckle. "I'm in charge of several age groups, so I'll be making the rounds while you're here. If you need me, I won't be far." She pointed to the door. "Just leave the top half of the door open and stick your head out. You'll probably see me rushing around."

"Okay," Brian said as he assessed the situation. "We'll be fine."

Kim immediately found herself surrounded by toddlers, all of them wanting her attention. To her surprise, Brian seemed completely at ease, making her wonder if something might be wrong with her.

"How do you do it?" she asked. "I've known you for— like—ever, and I had no idea you were a kid person."

"I have a baby brother, remember?" he reminded her. "And I used to have to entertain the younger cousins at family reunions."

Kim did remember him mentioning the family reunion thing. However, it hadn't really made an impact on her until now. Brian turned toward a little boy who tugged at his pants leg. Then as he leaned over, the child extended his arms to be picked up.

Carmen was by the door, watching. "Y'all will do just fine."

"Want me to read a story?" Brian asked Carmen.

"Sure, most of them really like to be read to," she replied. "Pick any book that looks good."

Brian nodded toward Kim. "Wanna pick me out a book? Make sure it's one with lots of colorful pictures."

She quickly chose one off the shelf then carried it over to where Brian had sat down, the little boy still in his arms. The other children took their places on the multicolored mat in front of Brian.

"Want Miss Kimberly to hold you while I read this story?" Brian asked the child still in his arms.

The little boy snuggled closer to Brian, making Kim feel terrible. "I don't think he likes me," she whispered.

"Oh, sure he does." Brian whispered something in the child's ear, and the little boy reached for Kim.

She took him as she gave Brian a questioning look. "What did you say?"

"It's our secret, right, buddy?"

The child offered a shy grin and nodded. Kim found a comfortable position on the mat, and a little girl climbed up beside the boy. She felt an unfamiliar emotional tug.

Brian warmed her heart as he read the book and showed the colorful pictures on each page. The children scooted even closer so they could see. When he finished the story, a couple of them hugged him. The sight of this still-in-shape, former high school football player and soldier being so gentle with all these toddlers touched Kim. It also made her realize there were some things she didn't know about him—mysterious things that attracted her in a way she never dreamed.

With each passing minute, Kim felt her emotions swirling in a whirlwind toward Brian, who captivated her not only with his love of sharing his faith but with his ability to relate to the children. She'd been thinking her feelings for Brian were displaced affection for David. But that wasn't the case anymore. As he patiently answered the children's questions, her heart felt like it would explode with love for him.

After Brian finished the last story, he tilted his head and gave her a questioning look. "Are you okay, Kim? You look like you don't feel well."

She licked her dry lips and nodded. "I'm fine."

The rest of the hour seemed to crawl, but eventually the adult Bible studies let out, and parents who'd been to the first service came by to pick up their children. One of them entered the room and informed Kim and Brian that they could leave because she and her husband were taking over.

"Are you sure?" Brian asked. "We can stick around awhile if you need us."

Kim wanted to kick him, but she faked a smile instead.

The woman shook her head. "No, that's okay. I know how exhausting it can be, and now it's my turn."

Carmen stopped by as she made the rounds between nursery rooms. "Thanks, you two. I don't know what we would have done without you."

After they were out of hearing distance, Brian laughed. "That wasn't so bad, now was it?"

"Bad?" Kim thought for a moment before shaking her head. "Not really bad but maybe a little scary at first."

"They're just little people."

"Little people who can reduce adults to bumbling idiots."

"Oh, come on, Kim. Admit it. You had fun."

She bobbed her head a little then smiled back at Brian. "It was okay. But you owe me."

"I owe you?" He tilted his head and looked at her. "For what?"

"For volunteering me to do something without giving me a chance to think about it or say anything."

"Oh, okay, I see how it is," he teased. "So what do I owe you?"

"I'll think of something good."

"How about I buy you lunch?"

She glanced at her watch. She needed to get away from Brian and try to sort out her thoughts. "Nah, that's okay. I need to get back and see if David responded to my e-mail."

Brian squinted his eyes and shook his head. "You have to eat. Let's go have some lunch, and then I'll take you home."

Kim felt her muscles tighten. She couldn't explain her need to put some distance between herself and Brian to recover from whatever was happening between them. He obviously wasn't going to let her get away with that.

"Okay, lunch," she finally agreed. "But my car is here." She'd have to work hard to keep an emotional distance—at least until she understood what was happening.

"Fine. I'll follow you home, and we'll go from there."

Fifteen minutes later, Kim's car was in her driveway, and she was about to get into Brian's car. He held the door for her then went around to the driver's side. Before Brian put the key into the ignition, he turned to Kim. "What're you in the mood for?"

"A huge stack of pancakes," she replied without looking at him. "Dripping with blueberry syrup."

"I know just the place." He drove straight to her favorite pancake restaurant where they served breakfast all day. "How's this?"

"Perfect." She hopped out of the car and met him around front, still avoiding his gaze. "Watching little kids really does something to the appetite."

"Wasn't Mackenzie cute?" he asked.

"They're all cute." Kim chuckled. "But you're right. I love that little curl on Mackenzie's forehead."

After the server took their orders, Brian studied her for a few uncomfortable seconds. Kim tried looking away, but when she turned back to him, he was still staring at her.

"What?" she asked.

"I was just thinking about how cute your kids will be. Have you and David talked about a family?"

She wanted to crawl under the table. How would she get through a conversation like this without breaking down and saying what she'd been thinking? "Not really," she replied softly. "We haven't even discussed the wedding, and that has to come first."

"Do you think you might want kids?"

"I haven't really thought about it," Kim said. "But I probably will. . .eventually."

Brian frowned. "You really need to bring all that out in the open before you settle on a wedding date. What if David doesn't want kids?"

Kim thought for a moment. "I'm pretty sure he does."

"You need to be totally sure. If one of you wants children

and the other doesn't, that's setting your marriage up for disaster from the get-go."

Kim played with her spoon for a moment as she thought about it. He was right, and she was dying to know if Brian wanted children. When she looked back up at him, he was still watching her. "Yeah, I guess we should discuss that when he comes back. How about you? I guess you probably want a house full of children."

Brian pulled back and made a face. "Not a houseful. Maybe two or three."

"You're so good with them, I thought you might want more."

"I'm good with a few at a time. I didn't mind this morning because I knew it was only for an hour or so, but if I had that many all the time, I don't know what I'd do."

"If your wife wanted a bunch of babies, you'd deal with it," Kim said.

Brian shook his head. "I'm not willing to just deal with it. I want the person I marry to be right for me in all the important areas. Not only does she have to love the Lord like I do, but she has to have similar values and expectations for a marriage and family."

Her heart thudded. She already knew that she and Brian had the same Christian values, and this conversation about children made her think about them. She had to find something that would get her mind back on the friendship track with him. "This isn't exactly a perfect world we live in, Brian. You can't place your order like that and expect to get it."

"True," he agreed, "but there are some things I feel are important to discuss. If my wife and I agree to have two children, and the second time she gets pregnant we have twins, I'll know that the Lord wanted us to have three children."

Kim had only eaten half her pancakes, but as Brian continued staring at her, she lost her appetite. "Can you take me home now? I really want to check my e-mail."

Brian paid the bill, and they left. Kim appreciated how he

didn't ask any more questions.

"It was fun," Kim said as she got out of the car at the curb.

"Wanna go to the singles Bible study next week?"

"I'm not sure." Kim held the door and thought about it for a second. "Call me tomorrow night, and we can talk about it."

As soon as she closed the door, he waved and took off. She went inside, kicked off her shoes, and booted up her computer.

Lord, please let there be an e-mail from David.

After clicking on her incoming e-mail, her heart grew heavy. Nothing from David. It wasn't as if he hadn't warned her, but she was still disappointed.

She was tempted to shut down her e-mail, find a good book, and read the rest of the day, but then she remembered how David said he enjoyed hearing from her daily—even if he got several days' worth of mail in one sitting. So she sat down and pounded out a letter letting him know about how Brian had hoodwinked her into working in the church nursery between services. She tried to keep it light and funny, but she kept thinking about what Brian said about children. So she added a few sentences at the end:

> *We've never discussed how many children we want after we get married. After hanging around with a bunch of active toddlers, I thought maybe it's something we should talk about. Would you like to have a couple of kids someday?*

Kim sat and stared at her e-mail before she clicked SEND. This might not have been the best time or way to bring it up, but Brian's comments would play in her mind until she had some idea of what David wanted.

❧

Brian felt bad about making Kim squirm, but as a friend, he felt it was his duty. He wanted to make sure she knew what she was getting into with David. The fact that David was so focused on the military concerned Brian—not so much that he wanted to serve his country but the fact that he made all his career decisions without consulting Kim.

Right.

To be totally honest, Brian knew his intensifying feelings for Kim made his motives not all that honorable. He still loved her as a friend, but it was so much more than that now. So much more romantic. Even after years of seeing her at her worst as well as her best, he loved everything about Kimberly Shaw, and it irked him that he hadn't acted on it before it was too late.

Time dragged by, but bedtime finally came. He fell asleep with Kimberly on his mind, and the first thing that popped into his mind when he woke up was their conversation at the pancake restaurant.

Brian reached for the phone but quickly yanked his hand back. He had to resist the urge to call her—especially this early in the morning. She worked long hours at the shop, and she might still be asleep since it was only seven o'clock. The Snappy Scissors didn't open until ten.

After drinking a cup of coffee and eating a piece of toast, he was on his way to the shower when the phone rang. It was Kimberly.

"Brian." Her shaky voice was barely audible.

He instantly went on alert. "What happened, Kim? What's wrong?"

"It–it's David. He. . ." She sniffled.

"I'll be right over. Just let me throw on some clothes."

five

The doorbell rang fifteen minutes later. Kim opened the door then gestured toward her computer. "His e-mail is still on the screen."

He started toward the computer, but suddenly he stopped. "I'd rather hear whatever it is from you."

Silence fell between them for a few seconds, but Brian didn't push. He patiently waited until she was ready to talk.

Finally, she faced him. "David doesn't want kids."

Brian frowned. "Are you sure?"

She nodded and pointed to the computer. "I wrote and told him about working in the church nursery; then I asked if he wanted to have children someday. He said he's never wanted to bring babies into this already overpopulated world."

"Maybe that's something the two of you should talk about in person instead of through e-mail."

Kim thought about it for a moment then shook her head. "What's interesting is that we don't really discuss all that much when we're together. We actually have more back and forth conversation in our e-mails than we do in person."

Brian held her gaze with a look of concern etched on his forehead. He patted her hand before pinching the bridge of his nose between his index finger and thumb.

"I know you're probably thinking it's my fault as much as it is his," Kim said, "and you're right."

When Brian didn't respond, she touched his arm but pulled away as soon as she felt the powerful pull she'd tried to resist. He repositioned himself to face her—and moved a few inches away as he looked her squarely in the eye. "Kim, you know how serious marriage is. After my experience, I've had quite a bit of time to think about it. If you don't talk—I mean really open up

48

with heart-to-heart dialogue—how do you know that you love each other enough to be husband and wife?"

She'd been asking herself that same question since David had been gone—especially after she realized her feelings for Brian had shifted. She'd wanted to discuss it, but now didn't seem like the right time.

"Kim, is there something else?"

She gave herself a mental shake, squared her shoulders, and bravely looked him in the eye. "It's weird. When David was here, everything seemed so good. Although we didn't have a lot of two-way conversation about the important stuff, he always talked to me about what he wanted, and it sounded really good. I loved the fact that he studied his Bible before making the commitment to Christ. With him, it was intentional and extremely well thought out."

Brian nodded. "Yes, I understand, and that's one of the reasons he and I are such good friends. When I was in the Guard, we had that to talk about. And we have sports in common. That's all we need to be good friends, but that's still not enough for a marriage."

"I know." She shook her head and fidgeted with the edge of her sleeve. Brian touched her cheek, and she turned to face him. "When he told me he was falling in love with me, I was caught up in the excitement of being half of a couple."

"There had to be more to it than that."

"Oh yeah, there's more. When he kissed me the first time, I got all tingly and silly. You know how it is." She flopped onto the sofa.

Brian snickered and sat down in the chair across from her. "Yeah, I know."

"It seemed that something exciting always happened when David was around. Between the kisses and his patriotism, I guess I just got caught up in my romance novel-style hero."

"I can see how that would happen," Brian said softly. "Do you regret being engaged?"

She closed her eyes. "Well, maybe. . .sometimes."

"You can't live your life like this, Kim. If you're not sure you want to marry David, it's not fair to either of you to stay engaged."

"I think I missed an opportunity to put our engagement on hold."

Brian lifted his eyebrows in surprise. "Opportunity?"

"I sort of had an opening before he left." Kim thought back and tried to remember precisely how it went, but she couldn't. "We talked about it. It seemed like he was thinking of me and my feelings, and I'm pretty sure he would have understood if I'd said we needed to wait."

"That's only right."

"I know." Kim swallowed hard then faced Brian again. "Oh, Brian, what should I do?"

He stood, placed his hands on his hips, shook his head, and offered a sympathetic grin. "With God, there are no shades of gray. I can't tell you what to do about something so serious." He pointed to the computer. "Why don't you write him back and let him know that the two of you have some things to discuss when he gets back?"

"I will."

"In the meantime, you need to think about why you're engaged in the first place. If you love him and think you can work through these issues, stay with him. However, if you don't think he'll take your feelings into consideration about some of life's most important events, like having children, you're setting yourself up for trouble."

Kim stood up and took Brian's hands in hers. "You are the best friend a girl could possibly have. Thanks. There's never been a time when you haven't been there for me."

"Yeah, I know." He suddenly sounded grumpy.

"Okay, what's wrong with you?" she asked. "I've been so wrapped up in my own feelings, I didn't even notice you were sad about something. . .until now. Is it Leila?"

Brian lifted a hand to wave off her concern. "No, it's not Leila. I'm fine."

"C'mon, Brian, I want to be here for you just like you are for me."

His eyes narrowed as he faced her head-on. "I didn't come here to talk about me, Kim. This was about you."

"But—"

"If you're okay now, I really need to get to work." He glanced at his watch and issued a mock salute. "We can talk later."

Kim blinked as he took off without another word. She had no idea what had just happened, but whatever it was didn't seem good.

She turned around and looked at the computer. The multicolored squiggly lines on the screensaver danced across the front of her monitor. She started to sit down and pound out another e-mail to David, but she decided to get ready for the day first to give herself time to think about what to say.

After she showered, dressed, and put on her makeup, she sat down at the computer. Even though Brian thought she needed to wait until David returned, she needed to get some things out now.

To: DJenner
From: KShaw
Subject: We need to talk

Dear David,
  I had no idea you didn't want children. I guess I just assumed you did because it seems like a natural progression after a couple gets married to want to start a family. I have to admit I hadn't thought about it until Brian and I worked in the church nursery.
  There are probably other things we need to discuss before we plan our wedding. I wish you were here so we could talk now. Have you heard anything about when you'll be coming home? I miss you.

Love,
Kimberly

She sat back and studied her note before she clicked SEND. Her letter wasn't flowery or gushy, but she didn't have much more to say, feeling the way she did at the moment. The clock on the computer let her know it was time to go to work. At least she had a full appointment book, so she wouldn't have time to think about what she'd just done.

❧

Brian's first goal when he entered his office building was to avoid Jack. He didn't feel like explaining anything to the only co-worker who seemed in tune to his life.

He slipped past the receptionist and made it to his office, thinking he was home free. But as soon as he unlocked his office door and entered, he heard the footsteps coming toward him. A quick glance up let him know he hadn't been successful.

"Hey, Brian. Don't forget we need six copies of that report—" Jack squinted his eyes, twisted his mouth, and studied Brian. "What's going on?"

"Nothing," Brian replied as he went around behind his desk. "I just had to run an errand this morning, so I'm a few minutes late. I need to print the report, and I should be good to go."

Jack hung back with his arms folded. "Are you sure you don't wanna talk about something?"

"Positive." Brian smiled. "Let me get everything together, and I'll be in the conference room in a few. We can go over it before the meeting."

"Fine."

Brian shuffled through a few papers while his computer powered up. As the report printed and collated, he prayed that he'd be able to focus on work and not his thoughts of yanking David by the collar for upsetting the nicest girl in the free world.

❧

Over the next several days with no response from David, Kim started getting worried. She called Brian, but he told her she should give her fiancé more time. Her mother reminded her that David wasn't always able to get online, so she shouldn't get all up in arms about a few days going by.

Then another week passed, and still no word, and she got worried. So she called David's mother.

"Hi there, Kimberly. I wondered if you'd ever bother calling me with David gone."

"I've been super busy with work and church. Sorry I haven't called sooner."

"Oh, I know how it is. I was young once." She exhaled loud enough to echo in the phone. "David seems to be doing quite well overseas."

"That's what I was calling about. I haven't heard from him in more than a week, and I was starting to get worried."

"You haven't heard anything? Oh my. I hope everything is okay between the two of you."

Kim paused. "Has he e-mailed you?"

"Why, yes, I heard from him last night. He told me he requested to stay an extra month so they could complete this mission." Before Kim could utter a word, Mrs. Jenner added, "You do realize how important my son is, don't you? I believe the security of our country rests in his hands."

"I know he's very important," Kim said as she tried to compose herself. David's mother obviously thought her son was single-handedly fighting for freedom. "Since I didn't get an e-mail from him, I thought maybe I'd missed his call because I've been sort of busy lately. I'm glad he's okay."

"Oh, he's fine. I'm sure he's even busier than you are, so don't worry about him."

"Well. . ." Kim racked her brain to find the right way to word what she wanted to say. Mrs. Jenner's condescending tone came across strong as ever. Kim found herself at a loss for words, because no matter what she said, Mrs. Jenner would cut her down to her knees. "Um. . .you're right. I just wanted to know if you'd heard from him."

"Okay, dear. Just don't forget how important this mission is. You're doing the right thing in staying busy. If he really needs to talk to you, though, he's not one to give up, even if you don't answer your phone."

When Kim hung up, she felt worse than before she'd called David's mother. David had once confided that his mother had gone to church on special occasions, but she never discussed a relationship with Christ. Church for her was more of an obligation rather than true, heartfelt worship. Until now, Kim thought that David might have misread his mother, but she didn't feel an ounce of Christian love or compassion from the woman. She sent another e-mail to David, asking him at least to let her know he was okay.

Kim continued her struggle with the combination of not hearing from David and the fact that Brian had started avoiding her. What was up with that? She'd called and left a message several days ago, and he hadn't bothered to return the call. That wasn't like him at all. Maybe he sensed that something about her feelings toward him had changed. To top it off, he hadn't asked her to go with him to the weekly singles Bible study since last time they went together. She worried that she might have scared him off.

"What's got you all in a snit?" Jasmine asked as they prepped their stations for the day.

"Nothing."

Jasmine paused, pulled back her chin, and lifted a severely tweezed eyebrow. "Don't try to pull that on me, girl. We've worked side by side long enough for me to know when you're out of sorts."

Kim laughed. "Yeah, I guess I'm out of sorts. . .a little. I haven't heard from David in a long time, and Brian's been avoiding me."

"I don't know David all that well," Jasmine said as she resumed arranging her combs. "But I know Brian well enough to advise you to call him."

Kim shrugged. "He's never home anymore."

"Then call him at work. You know he'll be there."

"I'll think about it."

Jasmine shook her head. "Y'all have been friends for a long time, Kimberly. This is silly."

Kim nodded her agreement. Jasmine was right. Finally, she grabbed her cell phone, went to the back room, and called Brian's direct line at work. His voice sounded weary as he answered on the first ring.

"I wondered if you were still alive," she said.

He cleared his throat. "Yeah, I'm alive. What do you need?"

In all the time Kim had known Brian, the only time she'd heard him so abrupt was when he broke his arm in the middle of football season and was mad that he'd been benched for the rest of the year. "Why don't you and I go out for pizza tonight?"

"I don't know, Kim. It might not be such a good idea for us to hang out so much."

So she was right. He was worried by the way she was acting. Kim resolved to get everything out in the open. "David told us to keep each other company while he was gone. He knows you and I have been friends for—like—ever. Where's the harm? I really need to talk, Brian."

Brian paused for a moment. "I guess you're right. You've always been there for me, so I'll be there for you."

"You don't have to make it sound like such a chore. If you don't want to talk to me, don't do it."

"Well, I'm not really in the mood to go out tonight. How about—"

"Then we'll just order in. You can come to my place. I really need to talk to you."

He cleared his throat. "What time do you want me there?"

His question came so quickly, Kim knew she'd played on his guilt and won. Suddenly she felt bad.

"Look, Brian, I didn't mean to pull a guilt trip. It's just that David hasn't even bothered to e-mail me. I called his mother, and—"

"Say no more. I've met her."

"Why don't you come over around seven? I'll order the

pizza after you get to my place."

"I'll be there," he said. "I'll bring the drinks. Cola or root beer?"

"Let's get crazy and have root beer."

Brian chuckled. "Sounds good. See ya tonight."

After Kim got off the phone, she put the phone in her pocket, rocked back on her heels, and thought about the differences between Brian and David. Brian had been brought up in a Christian home. David had come to Christ as an adult. When he made his commitment to the Lord, he turned his back on anyone who'd cause him to stumble, including his former girlfriend Alexis. Kim later learned that Mrs. Jenner and David's old flame had been very close, which explained the older woman's coolness toward Kim in the very beginning. David told Kim not to worry about that, but she couldn't help feeling bad about it.

She glanced up when Jasmine appeared at the door. "Your next appointment is here."

Kim took a step toward her. "Sorry about that."

"No worries. She just arrived." Jasmine paused and glanced over her shoulder. "You okay? I can get her started at the sink if you need a few more minutes."

"Nah, that's okay. I'm fine."

The afternoon was slow, giving Kim a chance to think even more about what was going on with David. By the time she left for the day, dozens of scenarios had run through her head.

When she got home, she showered to get rid of the chemical smells from the salon. Brian arrived shortly afterward, and she immediately placed the call to have the pizza delivered.

"Let me check my e-mail and see if David responded yet," Kim said.

Brian held her gaze for a moment before he nodded. "I'll put this root beer in the fridge while you do that."

Kim didn't expect a response this soon since she hadn't heard from him in so long. The instant she saw David's e-mail, her pulse quickened.

six

Brian took his time in the kitchen to give Kim some space. When he figured she had enough, he joined her.

"Any news?" he asked, trying to keep his voice steady.

Her shoulders rose as she inhaled, but she didn't say anything. This concerned him.

"What happened?" Brian urged.

Kim glanced down at the floor. "David heard from his mother, and he thinks I need to make more of an effort to get close to her."

Brian pulled a chair over from the dining table and sat down beside Kim. He took a moment to find the right words before speaking.

"What does he think you should do?"

She didn't meet his eyes for a few seconds. Then she turned to face him. "I have no idea."

Brian shrugged. "What does David have to say about it?"

"He's annoyed by her comments. I can't say I blame him, considering the life-and-death situations he faces on his job." Kim snorted. "I can't believe his mother is worrying him like this."

"Yeah, it does seem like she's got some issues that have nothing to do with you."

Kim smiled at him, warming him from the inside out. "Thank you, Brian. You're the most amazing man. Leila made a humongous mistake."

Brian allowed himself to get lost in a shared look between them, in spite of his internal alarms sounding off louder than ever. If only he'd acted when he still had a chance with her—before he introduced his two best friends—he might not be having this conversation.

As Kim turned back to finish reading her e-mail, he sank back in the chair and reflected. When they were kids, he was afraid of rejection, so he kept his feelings to himself, half hoping she'd give him a sign that she wanted more than friendship and half hoping his infatuation would fade. Now that they were adults, he saw the flaws in his earlier thinking.

A couple of times, he'd started to make his move, but the timing was never right. He wanted something special—a mood or setting they'd always remember. However, the couple of times he thought he'd arranged everything just right, someone else was always there.

When he'd brought David to church, it wasn't his intention to fix him up with Kim. However, David spotted something special in Kim, and he didn't waste any time.

Shortly after David and Kim met, Brian tried to see if she wanted more than friendship, asking her out and being there all the time. He actually caught her looking at him in a way that made him feel he had a chance. Then two sentences stopped him cold. She'd grabbed his hand and squeezed it before she said, "Thank you so much for introducing me to David. I think he's the one."

He'd stumbled and stuttered as he asked questions. "Are you sure? I mean, this is serious, Kimberly."

She nodded. "I'm positive. Last night he told me he loved me."

Brian was dumbfounded. Now that he looked back on that afternoon, he wished he'd said something—at least let her know how he felt. But now it was too late. Making moves on another man's fiancée wasn't the honorable thing to do. If nothing else, Brian Estep was an honorable man.

Kim clicked off the screen with the e-mail and stood up, jolting him from his thoughts. "The pizza should be here any minute. Let's go get our drinks while we wait." Some of the light he'd seen in her eyes earlier had dimmed.

He followed her into the kitchen. "Nothing from David?" he asked.

She shook her head. "Nothing important. Oh good, you

got my favorite kind." Kim pulled the two-liter bottle from the refrigerator. "Last time I had root beer was when I asked David to pick some up on his way here. Of course, there was no way he could know my favorite kind, and I didn't want to hurt his feelings. . ."

The more she talked, the more agitated Brian became. He knew what Kim liked because he'd actually listened to her all these years.

"I think you and David need to sit down and really get to know each other."

He saw Kim's jaw tighten. She gave him a look of annoyance. "We talk—just not about the same things you and I talk about. I know what he likes."

"Then why doesn't he know what your favorite root beer is?"

She snickered. "You're kidding, right? That's just root beer. Not important."

"Does he know that you like pink but you prefer peach?" Brian knew he was being ridiculous, but suddenly he didn't care.

"Come on, Brian. This conversation is getting silly."

"No, it's not silly. I just think it's time you and David sat down and had a heart-to-heart. I bet you know what his favorite color is."

She nodded. "He likes blue. Royal blue."

"His favorite drink?"

Without a second's hesitation, she blurted, "Dr Pepper."

"Okay, that's what I'm talking about. You know things about him because he does all the talking." Brian started pacing as thoughts raced through his head. "I've tried hard not to do this, but Kim. . ." His voice trailed off as he met her gaze. Before he melted and said anything he might later regret, he lifted his hands and let them drop to his sides, making a loud slapping sound on his thighs. "Never mind. I need to butt out."

Kim quickly closed the distance between them and gripped his upper arms as she positioned him to look at her. At first, he saw a tenderness in her expression, but she released her hold on him, glanced away, then turned back with a whole different look. "Brian, what you're doing is very sweet, and I appreciate it. You've been the best friend I've ever had, and I know you're looking out for me. But I'm a grown woman now, and I know how to take care of myself."

He had to use every ounce of self-restraint to keep from reminding her how upset she'd been earlier. Finally, when he was able to get a grip on his thoughts, he took a step back. "Yes, you're right, Kim. You are a grown woman. And I was right when I said I needed to butt out. Let's get our drinks now and go wait for the pizza." He started for the living room then stopped and turned to face her. "What kind did you order? Mushroom and olive for you or Canadian bacon for me?"

She rolled her eyes and grinned. "Half mushroom and olive, and half Canadian bacon."

That pretty much said it all. Kim was thoughtful to a fault, and it would be very easy for someone to take advantage of her. David was a great guy, but he wasn't right for Kim.

ða

Kim was relieved when the pizza arrived. It broke up their conversation, and she was able to steer it in a different direction without too much effort. She was getting weary of discussing David and his e-mailed reactions—especially since she had no idea what was really going on with him.

Brian hung around for another hour after they finished eating. Since they both had to work the next day, he gave her a hug and went home.

Kim stood at the door and waved as he backed out of her driveway. Once he was out of sight, she closed her front door and leaned against it.

Lord, I don't know why I get so confused when I'm around Brian. Maybe it's just because I'm lonely with David on the other side of the world. Or perhaps I'm worried that his mother will affect our relationship. Kim opened her eyes and pondered what to pray for before closing them again to continue.

Please give me some peace and protect David. Help me to keep my thoughts and feelings to myself so I won't worry Brian and scare him away from being my friend.

Kim went to bed and woke up still feeling unsettled. After she started the coffee, she resisted the temptation to reread David's e-mail. There would be plenty of time for that after work, and she didn't need to torture herself by trying to read between the lines. She wished Carrie was nearby to talk to.

Later that morning, Jasmine grinned at her as she walked through the door of the salon. Kim forced a smile back, but Jasmine could see through her. "What's wrong, Kim? Did something happen between you and Brian last night?"

"No, we just had dinner and talked." There was no point in letting on how confused she was about her feelings for Brian.

"I'm tellin' ya, girl, you need to take another look at Brian."

"And I'm reminding you," Kim said through a smile as she held up her hand and tapped her ring finger, "not to forget that I'm engaged."

"Which means you're not married, and it's not too late to change your mind."

Kim let out a nervous laugh. "When I agreed to be David's wife, I made a promise to always love him. Besides, I think this ring set David back a pretty penny."

"Trust me when I say that's nothing compared to what you'll pay if you marry the wrong man," Jasmine said. "I'm not talking divorce, either. Did I ever tell you about my cousin who regretted marrying the wrong man?"

"You mean the one who died young of a broken heart?"

Jasmine nodded. "Yeah, I guess I did tell you. Marianne was like you—a Christian woman who wanted to do the right thing, even if it meant being miserable."

"If she was so miserable, why did she marry the wrong man?"

"She thought she was in love with Paul in the beginning, so she took his ring. About three months later, she started to change her mind, but she was convinced it was just cold feet."

"Well," Kim said, "there is that."

"Yeah, but if your feet keep getting colder and colder, and not even thoughts of your wedding day can warm them up, you need to reconsider—or at least postpone the wedding until you're sure."

Kim thought about what had happened to Brian. "Yes, I can see your point."

Jasmine smiled. "I thought you might. I'm not asking you to break your engagement. All I want you to do is think about how you feel now and magnify that by at least ten. It doesn't get better after the vows."

"Thanks, Jas. I'll put more thought into it."

At the end of the long day, Kim went home with Jasmine's advice lingering in her head. She hesitated for a moment before turning on her computer. After the troubling conversation with Mrs. Jenner and frustrating e-mails from David lately, she felt conflicted about checking her e-mail.

❧

Brian sat down at the computer with a slice of cold pizza he'd brought home from Kim's the night before and a glass of root beer. He was surprised to see David's name on his incoming mail list.

> To: BEstep
> From: DJenner
> Subject: Coming home
>
> Hey, Brian. I need you to help me out with something. We finished our mission early, so I'm coming home.
> Here's where I need you. I want to surprise Kim. Do you think you can arrange a small get-together for family and close friends? I'd really appreciate it, buddy.
> Let me know as soon as possible, okay? Once my leave is confirmed, I'll let you know the dates. Thanks.
>
> Always,
> David

A surprise, huh? Brian read and reread the e-mail several times before he typed a reply.

To: DJenner
From: BEstep
Subject: Re: Coming home

I've known Kim most of my life, and she's not big on surprises. Why don't you tell her you'll be here, and we can just have a nice party with a bunch of friends?

Brian

By the time he finished checking the rest of his e-mail, he had David's response. He clicked on the subject and leaned back to read it.

To: BEstep
From: DJenner
Subject: Coming home

What are you talking about, man? All women love surprises. Kim just doesn't want anyone making a fuss over her. This is important to me, so do me a favor and help me out with this.

Always,
David

Brian hesitated for a few seconds before he clicked the REPLY button and typed his message.

To: DJenner
From: BEstep
Subject: Re: Coming home

Sure, I'll do it. Let me know the details when you have them.

Brian

After he clicked SEND, Brian sat back and thought about Kim and all the possible reactions she might have to a surprise of this magnitude. Would she be happy? He hoped so.

Was he happy? Nope, not at all.

When Brian had first met David during a two-week National Guard duty, he'd been impressed with David's focus and authority among his peers. His integrity had come through as unbendable. He seemed like a great guy, and Brian was happy to introduce him to all his friends at church. What he hadn't counted on was David putting all of his energy into sweeping Kimberly off her feet.

Kim was reluctant to get involved with David at first. From the moment Brian had brought David to church, he realized how powerful David's dark, brooding good looks were with the women. The minute David walked into the room, many of the single females became tongue-tied, or they made it obvious that they'd love to get to know him better. However, David instantly set his sights on Kim—perhaps because she proved to be the biggest challenge.

It took David several months of actively pursuing Kim before her guard came down. However, once he had that ring on her finger, Brian noticed the change in his friend. Kim seemed to have taken a backseat to David's passion for the military. When Brian confronted David, he got a lecture. He even tried to talk to Kim, but she reminded him that relationships required give-and-take—and she couldn't stand in the way of David's desire to do what he thought was right for his country.

Brian rose and carried his plate and glass to the kitchen. He needed to stop worrying so much about Kim and David's relationship. They were adults, and if either of them didn't like something, they were perfectly capable of changing it.

So what if his own feelings for Kim had changed? It was a moot point since she wasn't available.

He needed to find something else to get his mind off Kim. But first he'd have to honor his commitment to David on the party thing—even though David wouldn't listen to him about Kim hating surprises.

⠀⠀⠀⠀⠀⠀⠀⠀⠀⠀⠀⠀🙖

Kim checked her e-mail and spotted a message from David. This time, however, her pulse didn't quicken.

> To: KShaw
> From: DJenner
> Subject: Checking in
>
> Dear Kim,
>   How are you, sweetheart? I hope everything is going well back home.
>   We've gotten everything here under control—at least for now. After we tie up a few loose ends, I'm sure something else will pop up. I wish I could share some of my experiences with you. Maybe someday. . .
>   I've been thinking about getting you and my mother together so the two of you can get to know each other better. Due to the circumstances, it's been difficult. However, there's no doubt in my mind that my two favorite women will be the best of friends. I feel blessed to have both of you loving me and waiting so patiently while I help protect our country.
>   Tell Brian thank you for being such a gentleman and watching out for you. I owe him big-time. And I appreciate how much you've been able to help get him through the days following what he calls "the wedding that didn't happen."
>   I love you and miss you very much.
>
>   Your future husband,
>   David

Kim chewed on her bottom lip as she thought about David's e-mail. He said all the right things, but something about the tone of the message bothered her. She could be wrong, but it looked like he was leaving something out. Because she had harbored romantic thoughts of Brian, it bothered her a little to read his words of love.

The temptation to call Brian nearly overwhelmed her, but she resisted. There was no news—good or bad—in this e-mail, so what was the point? Brian was a busy man who'd shoved enough of his own life aside to cater to her moods. He'd always been there for her, and she knew he wasn't likely to stop anytime soon.

Too bad she couldn't be more like him. Brian not only lived his faith, but he accepted what Leila did without anger. Kim didn't think she could do that. The fact that her love for David had faded was proof.

☙

The next twenty-four hours were rough for Kim. She refrained from calling Brian every time her mood changed, and that was one of the most difficult things she'd ever done. It also showed her how much she'd come to rely on him.

She had just come home from work when her phone rang. It was Brian.

"Don't make any plans for three weeks from tomorrow," he said.

"Why?" she asked. "What's going on?"

"I'm, uh. . .having a little get-together for some close friends."

Kim picked up a pen and tapped it against the desk. Brian had an odd tone to his voice. "Are you okay, Brian?"

"Yes, I'm fine."

"So what's this all about? Your birthday isn't for a couple more months. Did you get a promotion?"

"Don't ask questions, Kimberly." He cleared his throat. "Just pencil me in on your calendar, okay?"

seven

Kim laughed. "Okay, consider it done, but only because it's you. Anyone else would have some explaining to do."

"So, how was work today?" he asked.

"Are you changing the subject?"

"Yes, and don't ask any more questions."

Again, she laughed. "Okay, okay, I won't. Work was fine. We've been busy—mostly with cuts. People aren't getting as many perms as they used to, and most of my customers are coloring their own hair."

"You never really did like working with chemicals, so that's a good thing, right?"

Kim knew he was avoiding something, so she played along. "Yes, it's a very good thing. I prefer cuts over everything else."

Silence fell between them for a couple of seconds. Normally, that would have been fine, but Brian cleared his throat, and her insides constricted.

"You and I need to talk soon," he said.

She forced a laugh. "You make it sound so serious. Why can't we talk now?"

"Maybe because it's too serious to discuss over the phone."

"C'mon, Brian, this is me. We've been through a lot together."

"Yes," he agreed as his voice lowered. "And that's what makes this so difficult. Mind if I stop by tomorrow night?"

"Sure, that's fine. Want to come for dinner?"

"No, I'll eat something before I come. I just want to talk."

After Kim hung up, an overwhelming sense of dread washed over her. She didn't want to keep worrying Brian with doubts about her relationship with David.

All night and the next day, Kim pondered what could be so serious that Brian couldn't bring it up on the phone. She felt Jasmine watching her until the last customer left. Jasmine finally laid down her scissors, turned to face Kim, folded her arms, and tapped her foot. "Okay, what gives?"

Kim avoided her friend's glare. "I don't know what you're talking about."

"You've been acting weird all day. Did David e-mail you with bad news or something?"

With a quick roll of the eyes, Kim shook her head. "No. In fact, he wants his mother and me to get together soon."

"Oh, that should be fun," Jasmine said with a wicked laugh. "Not."

"I'm sure we'll get along over time. It can't be easy for her to deal with her son getting involved with someone she barely knows."

"True," Jasmine agreed. "So why have you been so—I don't know—pensive all day?"

"I don't know how you can say that, Jazzy. We've had a steady stream of clients from the moment we opened."

"True, but you're still not acting like yourself."

Kim lifted her arms and splayed her fingers. "I can't always be Miss Suzie Sunshine."

Jasmine cackled. "You've got a point. Having your fiancé and best girlfriend leaving so close together must be hard."

"Yes," Kim agreed. "Very."

"Just remember that you can talk to me about anything. I've probably been through almost everything."

"Thanks, Jazzy."

Kim finished cleaning up and headed home, stopping off for a burger on the way. She didn't want to mess with cooking and cleaning, as eager as she was to find out what Brian wanted to talk about.

Time seemed to drag before he finally arrived. She flung open the door seconds after he rang the doorbell. Seeing him significantly brightened her mood.

"Whoa," he said as he lowered his hand. "You must have been standing right there."

"I was waiting for you," she admitted. "So come in and tell me what's going on."

Instead of heading for the living room, he turned toward the kitchen. She followed.

"Want something to drink?"

Brian shook his head and pointed to the kitchen chair. "Just sit down, okay?"

She silently obeyed. He was obviously in no mood for argument or ceremony.

As soon as she sat, he paced a couple of times. Suddenly he stopped, placed his hands on the back of the chair, and leaned forward. "Kim, I don't think it's right for you and me to. . . well, you know. . . ." His voice trailed off, but he continued staring at her.

"No, Brian, I have no idea what you're talking about." She frowned, and he remained silent. "What *are* you talking about?"

Brian pulled his lips between his teeth and looked down. When he lifted his head, he offered a half grin. "Kimberly, you're an engaged woman."

His closeness nearly took her breath away. "So? We've been friends forever."

"Well. . ." He took a step back and shook his head. "Things have changed."

"Changed? How?"

"I don't know. They've just changed."

"Have you met someone new?" *That must be it.* Disappointment shrouded her as she forced a grin. "You have a new girlfriend, and she doesn't understand about me. Want me to talk to her?"

"No, I don't have a new girlfriend. I haven't been anywhere to meet a girl."

"What's the problem, Brian?"

He lifted his hands. "I'm just not feelin' this whole friendship thing with you anymore."

Kim suddenly went numb. "Okay," she said, her voice

barely above a whisper. "That's fine."

Brian's stone-cold face softened, and he let out a snort. "It's not fine. I have to admit, I have feelings for someone, Kim."

Kim felt like her eyes would bug out of her head, and she had to steady herself. "So there is someone else—someone besides Leila?"

Brian hung his head. "Yes, I'm in love with someone else." When he looked back at her, a sad expression had clouded his eyes.

"Who?"

He pursed his lips and shook his head. "Can't tell you."

"That's insane, Brian. You can tell me anything."

"Nope," he replied. "Not this."

He'd rocked Kim's world way more than she ever thought he could. "Maybe it's just displaced feelings from Leila," she offered. "I'm sure that had a huge impact on you."

"Nope. It's the real thing. In fact, deep down, I think I was relieved when Leila didn't show up."

"That's crazy. Why did you get engaged to Leila?"

"The girl I love is off-limits."

Kim lifted her eyebrows. "Is she married or something?"

"Not married."

"Then she's involved with someone else?"

"Yeah, very involved."

"Like I said earlier, that's insane."

Brian chuckled and shrugged. "Probably, but it's the truth."

"Why have you never told me about. . .this girl you think you love?"

"There's no way you'll ever understand this, Kim."

"Then why did you tell me?"

"I thought you needed to know. From me."

"You're not going to get away with this, Brian," she said, forcing a smile. "This is me, remember?"

"Let's just drop it, okay?"

"That's impossible."

"Try, okay?"

She closed her eyes for a moment then opened them to find Brian staring at her. "You make me nervous just standing there."

He sat and fidgeted before looking her in the eye. "Now I'm doubting myself for telling you."

"You can tell me anything." She traced her finger along the edge of the table, trying to hide the jealousy that had bubbled inside her chest. "Why are you afraid to confide in me about this girl?"

"It's really complicated."

"And I'm pretty smart, ya know," she said. "Maybe I can help you figure out how to deal with things."

"There's nothing to figure out." He studied his hands before looking back at her. "So how are things going with David?"

"I told him we need to talk."

"That's good," Brian said. "At least it's a start," he said without an ounce of conviction in his voice. "I think it's best if I stay out of your relationship with David."

"Okay."

Brian had never acted this strange before, but it was obvious he wasn't going to fill her in on what the real problem was. Or who the girl was. Everything in her life suddenly seemed so off-kilter.

"So what now?"

"I bow out of your life—at least for a while."

Kim wanted to touch Brian, but she didn't dare. Instead, she stood and pushed her chair under the table.

Brian took the hint and got up. "I'd better head on home now." He turned and walked to the door but stopped and turned back to face her. "Kim, there is that little get-together in three weeks. I, uh. . ."

"That's okay, Brian. I understand if you don't want me there."

"No!" He spoke so quickly, it startled her. "I do want you there. You *have* to be there."

"But I thought—"

"There will be a lot of people, so it's different. You have to come." His gaze met hers. "Please?"

"Okay," she said, nodding her head.

"It's important." He frowned, adding to her confusion.

Kim held up her hands. "Okay, I'll be there. I just don't understand."

"You will," he said as he reached for the doorknob. "I'll see you around."

She stood at the door until he got in his car and pulled away. When she closed and locked it, she felt as though she'd just shut the door on the best friend she'd ever had in her life. How could such a solid friendship change so quickly and without her having a clue what had just happened?

❧

The next day, Brian stayed in his office with the door closed until Jack e-mailed him and asked where the report was. Brian shot him an e-mail right back letting him know it wasn't due for another couple of days. This elicited a return note, requesting an impromptu meeting ASAP. Brian wasn't in the mood for this, but he agreed to meet in the conference room in ten minutes.

This gave him time to say a prayer, grab the paperwork he had ready, and swing by the break room for a soft drink. Jack was sitting at the head of the table, waiting for him when he walked into the conference room.

"So what gives, Brian?"

Brian grabbed a coaster and carefully placed his soda on it; then he spread the paperwork out in front of Jack. He was about to sit down when Jack started laughing.

"What's so funny?" Brian asked.

"I didn't want to see all this." Jack gestured over the papers. "I just wanted to find out if you're okay. You haven't been yourself lately."

Brian raked his fingers through his close-cropped hair. "I've just been swamped with all the reports and—"

"Don't give me that, Brian. You can handle your job with your eyes closed. Something else is going on."

"Everything's fine."

"Okay, let me guess." Jack leaned forward. "Girl trouble?"

"C'mon, Jack, you know what happened. A guy can't get over being jilted this fast."

Jack tilted his head and folded his arms. "I don't think this is about Leila. It's Kimberly, isn't it?"

If Brian hadn't already confided in Jack when they first started working together, he would've been angry for the man sticking his nose where it didn't belong. He'd regretted it ever since.

"C'mon, man, that was a long time ago. David's coming home soon, and he wants me to have a party to surprise Kim."

Jack made a face. "David wants you to have a surprise party for him? That sounds rather presumptuous to me."

"Nah, it's not like that. He just wants to see some old friends, and while we're at it, we'll surprise Kim. That's all."

"Take some advice from a man with a few years on you, Brian. If you love Kimberly, and it looks like you still do, even though you refuse to admit it, don't stand back and let her go without a fight."

"David's one of my closest friends," Brian argued. "Don't forget I introduced them."

"That's beside the point. This is serious business. Your entire future is at stake."

"Thanks, Jack, but I'm fine."

"Kim's future is at stake."

Brian nodded. "David is a good man, even if he doesn't know how to show it. If anything, I should probably talk to him about improving communication with his future wife."

Jack leaned toward Brian. "Have you told her how you feel?"

"Discussion closed." Brian glared at his co-worker, willing him to stop pressing.

Jack stood, walked over to Brian, and placed a hand on his shoulder. "Man, I wish I could make things better for ya, buddy."

"I'm fine."

"Think about what I said. Have a talk with David. Let him know how you feel about Kim."

"Good-bye, Jack."

Jack snorted. "Okay, fine. Do what you need to do."

"Thanks." Brian smiled. "I appreciate your concern."

"Anytime," Jack said. "Today's meeting should be a barrel of fun." He rolled his eyes upward.

"I'm sure."

After Jack left the conference room, Brian stared down at the papers he'd brought. Until Leila stood him up at the altar, Brian was able to keep his feelings for Kim in check and his life mapped out in a very logical manner. However, that one act—or nonact—turned everything upside down.

❧

Kim couldn't put her finger on it, but she knew something was going on—some sort of secret. Everyone around her seemed to be in on it. Last time she visited her parents, they kept exchanging surreptitious glances. David's mother called and asked if she'd like to go shopping for a new outfit. Even Jazzy kept looking at her, snickering, and shaking her head, like she knew something but wasn't telling. Normally, she would have called Brian and asked him to help her figure things out, but after their talk, she knew she couldn't count on him to be straightforward.

Everything was just too bizarre.

Each day that passed brought even more strange events. She accepted David's mother's shopping invitation, and the woman insisted they go the following weekend. That never would have happened before, because every time Mrs. Jenner made an offer in the past, it was hollow, and nothing ever came of it. Jazzy grew silent and only smiled when Kim commented about David or Brian.

Then she called Carrie, who tried to get off the phone. But Kim wouldn't have it.

"Okay, what gives? Everyone's acting like I have a disease."

Carrie laughed. "I think everyone's just really busy."

"The people I want to see don't have time for me. But David's mother actually wants me to go shopping. I can understand everyone else being busy, but Mrs. Jenner hates me."

"Oh, I'm sure she doesn't hate you," Carrie said. "I bet David finally convinced her that you're a nice girl and that she really should get to know you."

"Oh right." Kim couldn't keep the sarcasm out of her voice.

"Guess what!" Carrie said.

"I can't imagine. What?"

"I'm coming home the day after tomorrow."

"Then let's get together this weekend."

Carrie cleared her throat. "Sorry, I can't."

"So what are you so busy doing?"

"I, uh. . .I have to clean my house."

"I've known you a long time, and you've never put a clean house before having fun."

Carrie laughed. "Okay, I'll level with you. Something is going on, but I can't talk about it now."

So Kim's hunch was right. "When can you talk about it?"

"Um. . .not for a while."

"Just answer me, Carrie. When?"

"How about a week from Monday?"

"Now that's just weird." Kim let out a sigh of frustration. "Looks like the only choices I have are to keep agonizing over this or coming over there and beating it out of you."

"Right. As if you'd ever resort to violence."

"Okay, so I'm not into using physical tactics. Just answer one question. If you don't tell me, will I ever find out what's going on?"

Without a second's hesitation, Carrie blurted, "Yes."

"When?"

"You said one question," Carrie said, "and I'm holding you to it. I have to go now. My boss needs to talk to me."

Next on Kim's list was Mrs. Jenner. She dreaded spending

a day of shopping with the woman, but since they would soon be related, she might as well start now. She opened her phone, scrolled through her list until she found Mrs. Jenner's number, and punched SEND.

eight

"Hello, dear," Mrs. Jenner said in a saccharine-sweet voice. "Why don't you plan for a full day of shopping. I want to make sure you get the perfect—" She suddenly stopped talking, as if she were afraid of saying the wrong thing.

"Perfect what?" Kim's radar was sounding an alarm louder than ever.

"Oh, never mind," the woman said with a giggle in her voice. This was so out of character for her.

"Okay, so what time did you want me to pick you up?"

"Are you sure you don't mind driving?" Mrs. Jenner asked.

"I love to drive."

"Then be here at nine thirty. The stores open at ten, and I want to get as much shopping in as possible."

Kim hated to shop, but if it would help her relationship with David's mom, she would sacrifice. "That's fine."

"And don't make plans for later in the day. I suspect we'll be out until dark, at least."

Kim held back a groan. "See you Saturday morning at nine thirty."

"That's right, Kimberly." Mrs. Jenner's stern tone had returned. "And don't be late. Punctuality is important to me. I'm sure David must have told you."

"Yes, I know that. I'll be on time."

After they hung up, Kim felt like she'd been through a wringer. She leaned against the storage room door and closed her eyes for a prayer.

Lord, give me the strength to endure shopping with Mrs. Jenner, and help me keep my thoughts to myself.

"Hey, girl, are you okay?"

Kim jumped back to the present at the sound of Jasmine's

voice. "Uh, yeah. Sorry. I just got off the phone with David's mom."

"I hope she appreciates the fact that you're taking one of your busiest days off work to spend time with her."

"Who knows what she appreciates?" *Sorry, Lord.*

Jasmine offered a sympathetic grin. "You'll be fine. If you want, I can call midafternoon and see how you're doing. There's always an emergency around here that can cut your time short."

"Thanks, Jazzy, but I need to do this. . .for David. He really wants me to spend some time with his mother, and I think I owe it to him."

With a smile, Jasmine nodded. "You're a very sweet girl, Kimberly. I hope David's mother will learn to appreciate you." She started to turn away but stopped. "Another thing. I've been wondering about Brian. I haven't seen him around lately. Is he doing better?"

"Yes." Kim heard the clipped sound of her response. She offered Jasmine an apologetic look. "At least I think he is."

"Okay, I get it. You don't want to talk about Brian."

Kim opened her mouth to explain, but she quickly snapped it shut. She was sick of talking about her feelings.

৵

Early Saturday morning, Kim got out of bed and examined the outfit she'd chosen for her shopping trip. It was a pink and black color-block dress with matching black flats and a pearl necklace—very safe and not something she'd normally choose. She'd bought the dress to go to one of her mother's events at church, and the pearls took on a completely different look when she wore them with jeans.

Dread filled her at the thought of wearing something she wasn't crazy about while pretending to enjoy shopping with a woman who didn't even like her. She trudged into the kitchen and got the coffee ready as she thought about what would make this day more tolerable.

For one thing, she could ditch the dress and wear pants

with a fun top. The ballet flats would work, and the pearl necklace would add enough sophistication to keep Mrs. Jenner from thinking she didn't care. Now she felt a little better about things.

However, that feeling was short-lived when Mrs. Jenner answered her knock. A quick once-over glance was a strong hint that the woman didn't approve.

"You're wearing *that*?"

Now she was certain Mrs. Jenner hated her. Kim forced her best smile and nodded. "Since we're making a day of it, I wanted to be comfortable."

"Comfort is all in the mind."

Kim noticed that Mrs. Jenner wore a black knee-length skirt, a ruffled white blouse, and a pink cardigan with tonal beading stitched into a floral design. "You look very nice," Kim said.

Mrs. Jenner's lips barely widened into a half grin. "In spite of what you must think, I'm comfortable, but since you've decided to be so casual, I might as well change."

"Oh no, don't feel you have to—"

"Sit down, Kimberly. I'll change into some slacks. It won't take long." She nodded toward the coffee table in front of the sofa. "While you're waiting, you might as well look through the photo album of David's life. I'm sure it'll give you some insight."

Kim did as she was told. As she flipped through the pages of the album, she saw a sweet little baby boy transform into the handsome man he was today. She knew he'd always been athletic, so she wasn't surprised to see him suited up in various team uniforms. However, when she got to the second to last page, she paused and stared.

There he was, wearing a tuxedo, standing beside a tall, dark-haired woman with dramatic eyes and a very curvy figure shown off by a glittery dress that looked as if it had been painted on her. Based on David's description of his former girlfriend, Kim knew this was Alexis.

Kim stared at the picture as a myriad of feelings flooded her. She was intrigued, amazed, and almost dumbfounded by the woman's exotic beauty. But not an ounce of jealousy surfaced.

"Looking at the snapshot of David and Alexis?"

Kim glanced up at her future mother-in-law, who hovered by the doorway. The only change she'd made was from her black skirt to some black slacks.

"Yes. He looks quite handsome in a tux."

Mrs. Jenner smiled as she crossed the room and sat in the chair adjacent to the sofa. "He certainly does. And get a load of Alexis. That is one beautiful woman. I don't know what. . ." Her voice trailed off as she shook her head and flipped her hand. "I guess you don't want to hear about the woman David almost married, do you?"

"I'm okay with it." Kim closed the photo album and squared her shoulders. Even to her, the fact that she wasn't jealous seemed really strange.

"Well, I suppose you have no reason to be bothered, since you're the one who caught the prize."

The way Mrs. Jenner had worded that, Kim felt as though she'd been in direct competition for David. But she hadn't. David and Alexis had broken up almost a year before Kim had even met him.

Kim stood and gestured toward the door. "Ready to go?"

Mrs. Jenner allowed a lingering, wistful glance at the closed photo album before closing her eyes and nodding. "As ready as I'll ever be."

"I thought we'd start at the mall," Kim said. "That is, if it's okay with you."

The woman shrugged. "That's fine. The mall's not a place I generally frequent, but I shouldn't expect a hairdresser to shop in the finer stores."

Kim's insides clenched. Until now, she could pretend that the only problem with her relationship with Mrs. Jenner was that they didn't know each other very well. Now she'd been verbally assaulted, but since she didn't know what to say, she didn't say anything.

After helping Mrs. Jenner into the car, Kim got in and drove toward the mall. Each time her future mother-in-law asked a question, she felt as if she were being interrogated in court. When Kim couldn't take it anymore, she maneuvered the car into an empty parking lot beside an office building.

"What are you doing?" Mrs. Jenner asked.

Kim stopped, put the car in park, then turned to face her fiancé's mother. "I know you don't like me, but don't forget, David and I are engaged to be married."

"Whatever do you mean, dear? Why wouldn't I like you? Is there something you're not telling me?"

"I know that Alexis is an attorney, just like David. I've known for a long time you wish he was still with her, but he's not."

"My son is a grown man. It's not my place to tell him what woman he should date."

"You seem to have a problem with me, and after that comment about my being a hairdresser—"

"It was simply an acknowledgment of what you do for a living."

That wasn't all it was, but Kim didn't want to continue with this confrontation. "Okay, fine. But I want you to know that I'm a very good hairdresser, and I have a large clientele who count on me to make them look good."

"I'm sure you do a very nice job with. . .hair."

Kim caught a glimpse of Mrs. Jenner in time to see the curled lip. She pursed her lips and said a silent prayer for the courage to make it through the day and the ability to keep from snapping. She bit back the words flitting through her mind as she drove the rest of the way to the mall.

The first couple of stores didn't have anything Mrs. Jenner liked, but the mall was big, and they hadn't covered even half of it by noon. Kim was getting hungry, but she wasn't about to be the first to bring up the subject of food after a comment

Mrs. Jenner had made shortly after they'd met. She actually asked Kim if all she ever thought about was her next meal.

"Let's see what they have here, then perhaps we can stop for a bite," Mrs. Jenner said as they approached one of the large department stores.

Kim nodded and followed the older woman toward the misses department. This wasn't a store Kim was familiar with. It catered to an older, more moneyed crowd. She gulped as she glanced at one of the price tags—way out of her price range.

As they approached one of the most hideous ensembles Kim had ever seen, Mrs. Jenner pointed to it and turned to Kim. "That looks like you. Let's find it in your size so you can try it on."

"I. . .uh. . ." Kim studied the bright purple sweater that topped a blouse that actually clashed with itself with orange and purple circles on an ecru background. She didn't want to insult Mrs. Jenner, but she'd never waste her hard-earned money on something like this.

"It's not my taste," Mrs. Jenner said, "but I know you like the. . .shall we say, bolder prints?"

Suddenly an idea struck Kim. "Why don't we find something that's not me? I think it's time to step outside the box."

She held her breath as David's mother pondered the point. Finally, the woman nodded and smiled. "Yes, I think that's an excellent idea." She placed her hands on her hips, scanned the racks, then gestured toward the door. "I'm getting hungry. Let's go grab something to eat, and we can talk about your makeover."

Kim didn't want a makeover, but who was she to argue? She dutifully followed Mrs. Jenner out the door and to the food court.

"I'm not used to eating like this," Mrs. Jenner said. "But I suppose when you shop at a mall, you're expected to eat. . . mall food."

The afternoon wasn't much better than the morning. Mrs.

Jenner shot down everything Kim liked. Finally, they agreed on a simple black knit dress with three-quarter sleeves for Kim. And to Kim's surprise, it was on a clearance rack. The only thing Mrs. Jenner purchased for herself was a silk scarf to go with something she already had.

All the way home, Kim listened to Mrs. Jenner talk about how they'd unearthed a treasure from the piles of rubbish. "I haven't done this kind of shopping in years—not since the early days of my marriage."

Kim pulled up in front of Mrs. Jenner's house and stopped. "Thank you for helping me pick out this dress."

Mrs. Jenner placed her hand on Kim's arm and offered a condescending smile. "We could have saved hours if we'd gone to one of my favorite stores downtown. Oh well, I suppose it'll make my son happy that we spent the day together." She got out and closed the door without so much as a good-bye.

"Yes, I'm sure it will," Kim muttered to herself as she pulled away from the curb.

When she got home, Kim hung the dress in her closet then changed into her jeans and sneakers. She was exhausted.

ఈ

Kim barely made it to church on time the next day, so she slipped into the back pew. Most of the time, she liked to sit closer to the front so she wouldn't be distracted by all the people.

As the congregation stood for worship songs, Kim found herself looking around for Brian. She didn't see him, but there were quite a few tall people between her and the front. She spotted Carrie in the second row from the front.

The pastor's sermon held her attention, but immediately after church, her mind flitted back to Brian. They normally went to the fellowship hall to hang out, but Kim wasn't in the mood to face Brian or Carrie today. Instead, she darted out the back door toward the parking lot. The sound of someone calling her name caught her attention, so she turned around.

When Brian didn't see Kim in church, he decided to forgo the usual coffee in the fellowship hall and just go on home. He spotted Kim practically running toward her car. She was obviously in a hurry, but he wanted to talk to her.

"Hey, Brian. I didn't see you in church. Did you want me for something?"

"Uh, not really." He shrugged and shoved his hands in his pockets.

Kim made a face. "If you hadn't lectured me about how you weren't 'feelin' our friendship anymore,' I'd ask you if you wanted to have lunch with me."

"About that. . ."

She folded her arms, tilted her head, and glared at him with a smirk. "Well?"

Brian lowered his head and stared at the pavement beneath him. When he looked back up at her, she was still in the same position, still staring, waiting. "Forget everything I said. It was stupid."

Kim tilted her head back and laughed. "Why is everyone acting so crazy? I feel like I've been abducted by aliens and dropped off at a planet of confusion."

Brian chuckled in spite of all the turmoil boiling inside him. "Let's have lunch together, okay?"

"Fine with me," she said. "Why don't we grab some deli food and head over to Magic Island? I haven't been there in a while."

Brian couldn't think of a more romantic place, but he didn't want to complicate things again. "Sounds good. Let me follow you home; then we can take my car."

All the way to Kim's house, Brian gave himself a mental lecture. He challenged himself to keep the conversation light and away from his feelings for Kim. Once they got there, she asked if he wanted to come inside while she changed.

"No, that's okay. I'll wait in the car."

"I'll hurry."

Brian shoved a CD in the car stereo and settled back to wait. When her front door opened, he glanced at her, and his heart thudded. Suddenly this didn't seem like such a good idea.

nine

Kim felt strange getting into Brian's car this time—especially after their last talk. He was still acting peculiar, too.

"So do you want the usual from the deli?" he asked.

She thought about it for a moment then shook her head. "No, why don't we shake it up a bit today? Blossom's isn't open, so we'll need to go to the grocery store deli. How about chicken and potato salad?"

"And maybe some baked beans," he added.

"You don't like baked beans," she reminded him.

He grinned. "I know, but you do."

"Okay, let's get some baked beans." Kim folded her arms and turned to stare out the front window. Normally she was fine with silence between them, but even a few seconds of quiet felt wrong. "So how's work?"

He shrugged. "Same. How's the hair business?"

"Good." Kim couldn't stand it any longer. "Okay, Brian, this is crazy. You and I have never been like this before."

"Like what?" He stopped for a light and cut a glance her way.

"You know, like a couple of dorky teenagers who don't know what to say to each other."

Brian tilted his head back and laughed. "Now that's a good one. We might not be teenagers, but we have every right to be as dorky as we want."

Kim grinned back at him. "Okay, now that's better. Do me a favor, okay?"

"I'm not making any promises until you tell me what it is."

"Let's try to get back to the way we were."

He hesitated before nodding. "Good idea."

"I'm starving, so let's get a family-size order of chicken."

He chuckled. "That's the Kimberly I know."

86

They were in and out of the grocery store in fifteen minutes, on their way to the Magic Island Park. As Kim spread the blanket on the grass, Brian dug through the sports equipment box in his trunk and pulled out a Frisbee and a foam football.

Kim had a wonderful time relaxing after lunch. Brian gave her just enough time for lunch to settle before he jumped to his feet and extended her a hand. "Ready to toss the Frisbee?"

"Sure," she replied as she stood. "I can't believe how gorgeous it is today."

Brian's expression grew pensive. "Yes, it is gorgeous, isn't it?"

The best thing about throwing the Frisbee with Brian at that moment was the distance between them. Kim sensed that at times he was uncomfortable. She had to do something to relax him.

She'd just missed the Frisbee to the sound of Brian's laughter when a solution hit her. He'd fixed her up with David, so she could return the favor and introduce him to some new people. Even if he didn't fall in love with one of them, it would get his mind off the off-limits woman—whoever she was. There had to be some nice Christian girls who'd love to date Brian.

They played for more than an hour before Kim held up her hands. "I need to get back home."

Brian checked his watch. "It's still early."

"Tell that to the mountains of laundry piling up beside my washing machine."

He snorted and tucked the Frisbee under his arm. "You win."

As they rounded up the trash and carried it to the bins nearby, Kim chattered about how much fun she'd had. Brian didn't speak until they got back to the blanket, where all they had to do was stuff the food into the basket and carry it to the car.

"You are still planning to come to my party, right?"

"Of course I'll be there." Kim felt terrible that she'd forgotten about it. "Can I bring anything?"

Brian's eyes twinkled at first then dimmed as he slowly shook his head. "No, I have everything covered."

"I don't mind bringing a bag of chips or some dip or something."

"It's not that kind of party," he said. "It's a little. . .well, nicer."

"What do you mean?" Kim stopped in her tracks and stared at Brian.

"I don't mean anything other than the fact that I've decided to have a party where people dress up and we actually eat decent food."

Kim laughed. "Like what? Caviar?"

"Maybe."

"That's so not you, Brian."

"What? Are you saying I don't have class?" He gave her a mock hurt look.

"Oh, you have class, but as long as I've known you, you've been a chip and dip kind of guy."

He unlocked his trunk and dumped the sports equipment into the box. "And look where that's gotten me. I'd say it's time for a change."

All the way to Kim's house, she tried to talk him into having a more casual party. "Your friends don't care if you're not fancy, Brian. Don't stop being yourself." She narrowed her eyes as she remembered his comment about his complicated feelings for the girl. "Are you trying to impress someone?"

"No," he snapped. He stared straight ahead, not even casting a glance her way when he came to a stop and put his car in park. "You can't change my mind."

Kim grunted. "So you're saying I have to dress up?"

"Yes."

"That's just plain silly."

Brian's lips twitched, but he didn't smile.

"What's going on, Brian?"

"I already told you. I'm having a dress-up party. We're adults now. It's time we acted like it."

Kim couldn't help but howl with laughter. "Who are you? Where did you put Brian?"

He turned to face Kim. "Do me a favor, Kim, and stop asking questions. Just come to my get-together in something nice. You'll understand later."

The seriousness of his expression let her know it was time to quit arguing. He wasn't playing games. This whole dress-up party thing was for real—and it was important to him. But why?

"Will your boss be there?" she asked.

"Uh-uh-uh. No questions, remember?" He wiggled his index finger in the air. "Now go on inside. I have stuff to do to get ready for work tomorrow."

Kim nodded and opened the door before something dawned on her. "Wait a minute. I was the one who had stuff to do. You wanted to stay later."

"You reminded me of laundry."

She laughed. "Okay, Brian. I'll leave you alone about this party thing. If you need help with it, just let me know."

"What would you know about a fancy party?" he teased.

"About as much as you." She winked and grinned as she shut the car door.

Once she got to her front porch and unlocked the door, she turned and waved. Then she went inside. Yes, it was definitely time to introduce Brian to some new people. Since he was ready to move on, and she couldn't have him, perhaps she could find someone to make him happy. That thought made her stomach hurt, but she was so confused, she couldn't think of another solution.

First, she called Carrie and told her the plan. "Good idea," Carrie said. "But who do you know that Brian doesn't?"

Kim tapped her pencil on the table and thought. "I have a few customers he might hit it off with."

"Are they Christians?" Carrie asked.

"One is for sure, but the other two I'll have to ask."

"So, smarty-pants, how do you plan to execute this scheme?"

"That's why I called you," Kim replied. "I figured you could help me out with this."

"What makes you think I'd want to be involved in something so underhanded?"

Kim pretend gasped. "Underhanded? *Moi?* No, I'd never resort to underhandedness. All I want to do is help Brian like he helped me."

Carrie chuckled. "Since you put it that way, I'll look around and see if I can think of someone good, too."

"Perfect. Brian will probably be okay with one or two introductions, but we can't force too many on him too quickly."

"I agree," Carrie said.

"We'll each make a list and get together later—that is, when you have time—to put them in order of how we think they'd get along."

"No problem, I understand. I'd like to hang out with you and plan Brian's future, but let's wait until after this little party of his."

Kim chuckled. "I don't know if that can wait. Oh, speaking of the party, do you have any idea what's going on with him? He told me I have to dress up."

"Yeah, I know," Carrie agreed. "It's weird, isn't it?"

"Even worse, he told me he's not serving chips and dip. It's. . ." Kim cleared her throat and deepened her voice in a hoity-toity tone. "It's a party where people dress up and eat fancy food."

Carrie giggled. "Did he actually say that?"

"Yes. Something is definitely going on."

"I'm sure."

"You don't know something I don't know, do you?" Kim asked. "I mean, has anyone from church mentioned anything about this party. . .besides Brian?"

"Um. . ." Carrie coughed. "Look, Kim, I really need to run."

"Wait—"

"See ya." *Click!*

Kim held out the phone and stared at it before placing it in the cradle. One minute Carrie was with her, and the next minute she was back to acting just as strange as Brian.

Kim worked on involving Jasmine in her plan to find some-one suitable for Brian. At first, Jasmine balked.

"I don't think this is such a good idea, Kim," Jasmine said. "If you take a step back, you might see that he holds every woman up to you, and there's no way anyone can withstand that."

"Don't be silly," Kim said. "He's just lonely and floundering after what Leila did."

"Well, if you want my opinion—even if you don't want my opinion, Leila did him a huge favor. He wasn't in love with her."

"Oh, I'm sure he loved her," Kim argued as she thought about his confession. "But you're right. She did him a favor." She didn't mention how he'd found someone else to love— the complicated relationship with the woman he wouldn't even discuss with her.

"There's a difference between loving someone and being in love." Jasmine nodded toward the door. "We can resume this discussion after work."

Not only did they resume their discussion after work, but they talked about it every morning and afternoon, until finally, Jasmine relented. "Okay, if you're going to be that stubborn about it, I'll keep an eye open for a nice girl for Brian. Just remember it was your idea."

Kim smiled. "I'll take credit for it when he finally meets the woman of his dreams."

Jasmine shook her head. "That's the problem, Kim. He already has."

ten

"You what?" Brian couldn't keep his voice down. Had Kimberly lost her mind?

"Calm down, Brian."

"How can I calm down with you trying to play matchmaker?"

He heard her quick intake of breath over the phone line, letting him know she was startled by his reaction. "I'm not being a matchmaker. I just want you to meet this girl. She's very nice."

Brian forced himself to lower his tone. "I'm sure she's a very nice girl. Probably the nicest in all of Charleston."

"Just do me a favor and meet her. I'm not asking you to marry her."

"No, but that's probably next on your list of things to do."

"Look, all we'll do is get together for pizza or something—"

"What, you, this girl, and me?"

"I was thinking the singles group from church."

Brian snickered then dropped his voice to a growl. "So you want to involve everyone we know? That's not gonna happen."

"How about lunch sometime? That way, you'll have a set amount of time and a good excuse to leave."

"Just the three of us?"

"Yep. You, Michelle, and me."

"Fine. We'll get together for lunch." He figured he might as well give in, or she'd bug him until he did.

"How about Thursday, eleven thirty, at Blossom's?"

Brian laughed. "You little schemer. You had this whole thing set up, with every last detail already planned, didn't you?"

"Well. . ." Kim cleared her throat. "You'll really like her, Brian."

"So you said. Okay, but if this is as big of a disaster as I think it might be, you have to promise never to do this kind of thing again."

Silence fell between them.

"Kim, did you hear what I just said?"

"I'm thinking."

"Promise you won't try to fix me up after I meet Michelle."

"Oh, Brian, I can't make that kind of promise."

"That's what I thought." He decided to change the subject. "So have you thought about what to wear to my party?"

"Your fancy-schmancy, hoity-toity party where everyone has to dress up and eat pretentious food?"

"That's the one."

"I bought a black dress I didn't need when David's mother and I went shopping, so I'll probably wear that, just to get my money's worth."

"Excellent," Brian said.

"I don't know why you sound so down about it when you're the one who came up with this harebrained idea to be something you're not."

"I know," he said. "It was probably a huge mistake."

"So now you're going for drama? Brian, you're such a goofball. Anyway, we'll see you on Thursday at Blossom's. Why don't you wear that light blue dress shirt instead of a stark white one?"

"Okay, I'll wear whatever you want me to," Brian agreed. "I've already learned there's no point in arguing with you."

"Smart boy."

After they got off the phone, Brian hung his head and closed his eyes. *Lord, get me through lunch on Thursday and the party for David, and keep me from making a fool of myself either time.*

"Hey, are you okay?"

Brian opened his eyes just as Jack sat down in the chair across from his desk. "You have great timing."

Jack made a face. "Seems like there's never a good time for you anymore. What's going on now?"

"Kim's trying to fix me up with some girl."

"And you're complaining?" Jack leaned back in the chair, folded his arms, and crossed his legs. "Kim knows you well enough to know what you like." He tilted his head and squinted. "Maybe that's what you need."

"Nah, I don't think so. Getting fixed up is not my thing."

"According to the experts, it's the best way to meet people. They've been prescreened by your friends."

"I don't need Kimberly Shaw prescreening my dates."

Jack chuckled softly but stopped when Brian glared at him. After a couple of seconds, Jack stood. "If I were you, I wouldn't turn down any opportunity to meet people. You never know what might come of it." He took a couple of steps toward the door, turned to face Brian, and shook his head. "On second thought, maybe you're better off not meeting people."

"Why do you say that?" Brian asked.

"You might find someone you like, and then you'd have to risk meeting the real Ms. Right."

Brian lifted his hands and looked up at the ceiling. "It's a conspiracy, I tell ya."

"Yeah, a conspiracy to get our friend back to the living."

"Okay," Brian said as he escorted Jack to the door. "Point taken. Now I gotta get back to work."

&

Michelle shifted in her seat. "Are you sure he agreed to do this?"

"Positive," Kim said, trying to sound more sure of the situation than she really was. When she'd first planned the meeting, it seemed like the right thing to do, but now she wasn't so sure. Deep down, she was conflicted over her own feelings for Brian.

"What if he doesn't like me?"

Kim turned to face her client of two years. "What's not to like, Michelle? You're very sweet, you're pretty, you're smart, and you love the Lord."

Michelle tilted her head and glanced down at the table

before looking back up with a shy smile. "Thank you for saying such nice things, but you know as well as I do that there's more to people liking each other than all that."

"Maybe so, but it's a good start." Kim spotted Brian as he walked in the door, so she lifted her hand and waved. "Over here, Brian!"

Michelle cast a glance over her shoulder then turned back to face Kim. "He's cute," she whispered.

"Told you." Kim smiled at Michelle as she waved him over. "Brian, I'd like for you to meet one of my favorite clients, Michelle."

Brian extended his hand and tipped his head forward. "Nice to meet you, Michelle. Kim has said some very nice things about you."

"Aren't you gonna sit down?" Kim asked, pointing to the chair.

Brian grinned at Michelle then turned to Kim with a teasing glance. "I need to talk to one of my buddies I haven't seen in a while. Do you mind ordering for me?"

"Of course not." Kim said. "Want the usual?"

As soon as he left the table, Kim turned back to Michelle. "Well, what do you think now?"

"He's very nice." Michelle rested her elbow on the table then propped her chin on her hand.

"But?" Kim sensed her friend's reservation.

"I saw the way he looked at you." Michelle frowned. "Are you sure there's nothing going on between the two of you?"

"Oh, come on, Michelle. You know I'm engaged. Besides, Brian and I have been very good friends for so long, we're like brother and sister."

"I know, but—"

"Anything but friendship with Brian would be flat-out creepy."

One of Michelle's friends walked up to the table. After Kim met her, Michelle and the other woman chatted, giving Kim a chance to think. She decided that she needed to look at Brian less and focus on everyone else more.

Shortly after Michelle's friend left, a server came to take their order. By the time Brian came back, their drinks had arrived.

Brian turned his attention to Michelle. "Are you from West Virginia?"

She nodded. "Yes, but I'm originally from Huntington."

"So what brought you to our lovely town of Charleston?"

"My job."

Kim piped up to help out. "She manages a fashion store."

Brian lifted his eyebrows and nodded his approval. "Managing a store is hard work. Do you like your job?"

"I love it," Michelle replied. "I've always enjoyed fashion."

An unexpected pang of jealousy shot through Kim as she watched Brian give Michelle a once-over glance. "Yes, I can tell you're very good with fashion."

They chatted throughout lunch, until finally, Kim couldn't handle the situation anymore, so she stood up. "Well, gotta get back to work. I have an appointment in about fifteen minutes. It's been fun."

Brian lifted his hand in a wave. "See ya." Then he turned to Michelle. "Can you stick around and talk for a few more minutes?"

Michelle's face lit up. "Sure!"

"You two have fun." Kim paused with a forced grin then turned and left.

All the way back to the shop, she gave herself a mental lecture. What was going on with her? Not only had she and Brian been friends forever, she had a fiancé, and she'd been the one to introduce Brian to Michelle. Why did she have such an unsettling sensation in her stomach? The better question was why did she have to have these feeling for Brian and complicate things?

The second she shoved open the door to the shop, Jasmine's eyebrows shot up. "Whoa, what happened to you? Did one of them not show up? Don't tell me Brian chickened out." She contorted her mouth before continuing. "Did Michelle change her mind?"

"No, they were both there," Kim replied without stopping on her way to the storage room.

She heard footsteps and wished she'd been better at hiding her feelings. Talking to Jazzy right now was the last thing she needed.

Fortunately, the bottles of color were on the far shelf, so she had her back to the entrance. But she could still hear her co-worker.

"So what happened that has you all in a snit?" Jazzy asked.

"I'm not in a snit. I just had to rush to get back before my appointment arrived." She perused the color for a moment. "Have you seen the dark golden blond?"

"To your right, where it always is."

"Oh, okay, thanks." Kim pulled the bottle off the shelf and loaded her arms with the rest of what she needed.

"You don't wanna talk about it yet, huh?"

Kim turned to face Jasmine. "There's not much to say. Michelle and I got there first, then Brian showed up. We talked over lunch, and I had to go." She swallowed hard. "They're still at Blossom's."

Jasmine turned her head slightly without taking her eyes off Kim. "And this bothers you, doesn't it? I was afraid of that."

She shrugged. "Why should it bother me?"

"You are in such denial, girl. Trust me when I tell you what's obvious to other people. You're conflicted between Brian and David."

Kim hung her head and let her shoulders sag. "I don't know why I feel the way I do."

Jasmine closed the distance between them. Kim leaned into her as she felt her caring friend's arms envelop her. "David's been gone for a while, and Brian's always here, that's why."

"So I need to keep praying for David's overseas tour to end, and everything will be fine, right?" Kim looked into Jasmine's eyes, hoping to see agreement. But she didn't.

"Who knows? Sometimes it's not that easy dealing with matters of the heart."

"Have you ever felt torn like this?"

Jasmine nodded. "Yes, several times."

"What did you do?"

"When I was a teenager and in my early twenties, I played the field. But when I got older and realized that wasn't good for anyone, I spent some time alone to figure out what I really wanted."

Kim snickered. "I've spent way too much time alone, and I think that's part of my problem."

"Just remember what I keep saying—that you're not married yet. After David returns, you can see how things go with him. The Lord will work this out in His own way. Try praying about it and leave the rest up to Him."

With a nod, Kim headed for the door. "You're right. I need to stop trying to figure everything out by myself."

The timer at Jasmine's station dinged. "I need to finish up with my client. We can talk later."

Shortly after that, Kim's client arrived, and both hair-dressers were busy for the remainder of the day. Jasmine's husband came to pick her up because her car was at the shop.

"Hi, Wayne. Jasmine's in the back. She'll be right out."

"Hey, Kimberly," Wayne said as he plopped down in his wife's chair. "You're lookin' good."

"Thanks," Kim said. "So how's everything at the auto shop?"

"Going great! Business is better than ever now that people are hanging on to their cars longer." When his wife came back, Kim noticed the spark between them.

"I'll finish up here," Kim offered.

"Don't forget what I said."

"Trust me," Kim replied. "I'll be thinking about it all night."

After Jasmine and Wayne left, Kim swept the shop, put everything away, and headed home. As soon as she walked in, she sat down at the computer to check her e-mail. It had been a while since she'd heard from David, and she was surprised there was an e-mail from him.

To: KShaw
From: DJenner
Subject: Thanks!

Kimberly, sweetheart, Mom told me you spent the day with her. I'm so happy my favorite girls got to spend some time together. Remember I said you'd love her after you got to know her? I'm sure that over time you'll become the best of friends.

I'm counting the days until I come home. So far, the mission has been successful.

Tell Brian I want to challenge him to a game of golf when I get back—that is, after my knee heals. I'll tell you all about it later. But don't worry. It's nothing permanent.

I love you, Kimberly. I know you're probably eager to start with wedding plans. As soon as I know something, we can talk about it.

Until next time.

Love,
David

Kimberly sat back and reread the e-mail a couple more times. She wished David had been more concrete about when he was coming home, but not even an ounce of disappointment had broken through the shell of numbness that surrounded her. He'd mentioned his knee needing to heal, so she wondered about that.

ro

Michelle was a very pretty woman, and she was nice enough, but Brian couldn't see himself falling for her. After Kim left, he tried to force himself to focus on Michelle, but his mind kept wandering to the picnic with Kim at Magic Island.

After he left the office, he stopped off at the store and picked up a few frozen dinners. He knew he should eat healthier, but he wasn't motivated to cook full single meals. Besides, he had a big lunch, and he wasn't even hungry yet.

After unloading the groceries and putting them away, he checked his e-mail. He'd been expecting to hear back from David, who was obviously too busy to reply to his question about the details of the big homecoming.

David's e-mail popped up. Finally. It was about time.

To: BEstep
From: DJenner
Subject: Our surprise

Hey, Brian! How's it going, buddy? Mom sent me a note letting me know she helped Kim pick out a pretty dress for my homecoming. I'm sure she'll be gorgeous as usual.

I just wanted to confirm my arrival. I'll be at my mom's place at 1800 hours on Friday night. She didn't think it would be a good idea to go to my apartment until after the party, in case Kimberly drove by. Mom said Kim's been moping around. What can I expect? I suppose my absence has been rough on her.

Saturday morning I'll swing by your place and help you with the finishing touches. I want this to be the best surprise ever for Kim.

You don't have to reply to this. I just wanted to confirm. See you soon.

David

Brian's jaw tightened. So David's big homecoming was actually going to happen. A shroud of disappointment fell over him. Then his phone rang.

eleven

Brian glanced at his caller ID and saw Kim's name and number. He stared at it for a second before answering.

"So did you make plans with Michelle?" she asked, her voice light and lilting—and very unnatural sounding.

"Um. . .no."

"Huh? I thought you two hit it off."

"She's a very nice girl."

"But?"

Brian cleared his throat. "She's really not my type, Kim."

"What, exactly, is your type?" Kim sounded annoyed, but that was too bad; he was annoyed, too.

"I'm not sure."

"Then I'll keep trying."

"Look, Kim, I appreciate what you're doing, but if and when I decide it's time to jump back into the dating pool, I can find my own women."

"That would be fine, Brian, but there's just one problem."

So now she was going to tell him what was wrong with him? "And that is?"

"If you want to meet someone new, you have to go places where the nice girls are."

Yeah, that was true. "Maybe someone new will show up at church."

"Maybe so, maybe not. What if I just happen to meet some really cute, single, Christian girl at the salon? Wouldn't you rather I introduce you to her than leave you to wander around trying to figure it all out?"

"Figure what out?" Brian asked. He couldn't keep the grumpiness out of his voice.

"How to meet girls. Isn't that what we were talking about?"

"That's what *you* were talking about, Kim. I'm just the innocent bystander in this situation."

She laughed, which irked the daylights out of him. Brian found himself getting annoyed much more frequently these days.

"Innocent bystander, huh?"

"That's what I said." He felt his jaw tighten. "So why don't we forget about fixing my love life for a while and talk about something else?"

"Okay. Did you think of anything I can do to help you with this get-together Saturday night?"

"Nothing. Everything's all set."

"You have all the drinks and food? How about music and games?"

Brian could tell she was hurt, so he quickly came up with something. "Why don't you bring one of your group games?"

"Okay!" she said. "See? I knew there was something you'd forgotten."

"Thanks, Kimberly. Now I really need to run."

"Oh, one more thing I almost forgot to tell you. I finally heard from David."

Brian tensed. "Anything I need to know about?"

"Not really. He just said he wants to challenge you to a game of golf."

"Sounds like fun." But it didn't really.

"Are you okay?"

"Yeah," he replied. "I've just had a really long day."

"I guess I'd better let you go then. See you Saturday night?"

"Yep. See ya then."

❧

Kim was tired of being in limbo. She was ready to get on with her life. And her moods were getting worse every day. She stormed into the salon the next morning. "I don't get why David bothered getting engaged if he planned to go on special missions."

Jasmine had a quick answer for that. "I think he just

wanted to stick that ring on your finger to let all the guys know you're off-limits."

"All the guys, huh?" Kim snorted. "It's not like I have a bunch of them standing in line."

"That's your own fault. Why don't you e-mail David and tell him you're not going to wait around forever?"

Kim tilted her head forward and gave Jasmine a hooded look. "The man is over in the Middle East fighting for peace, while I'm here in the cushy United States, complaining like a brat. How can I do something like that to him?"

Jasmine rolled her eyes. "You're not acting like a brat. He should have waited to propose. What he did to you was very unfair."

"He didn't do anything to me," Kim retorted. "I didn't have to accept."

"Then tell me this. When he asked you to marry him, did he first tell you he was planning to request to be assigned to this. . .special mission?"

"No."

"Would you have agreed to take his ring if you'd known?"

Kim paused and lowered her gaze. "I'm not sure."

"There ya go. He withheld information, so I think you have good reason to break off the engagement—or at least postpone it."

Jazzy had a valid point. "Maybe so, but I don't know about doing it via e-mail."

"How else can you do it?"

Kim lifted a shoulder and let it drop. "That's the problem. The only way we communicate is through e-mail."

"Maybe something will come up." Jasmine quickly turned away.

"What do you mean?"

"I don't know. Perhaps you'll figure something out soon."

"Yeah," Kim said with a snort. "I'll just hop on a plane and have them fly me to the Middle East. Maybe I can stay at a luxury resort and make a vacation of it while I'm there."

Jasmine lifted an eyebrow and shook her head. "You don't have to resort to sarcasm, Kimberly. It's not becoming."

"Now you sound like my mother."

"Speaking of your mother, have you talked to her lately about all this?"

"No." Her mother loved both David and Brian, and Kim didn't want to discuss her confusion until she had things sorted out in her own mind. But it would be nice to see her parents.

"Your mother is a wise woman. Perhaps she'll have some insight that might help."

"Maybe," Kim said. The bell on the door jingled from the sound of Jasmine's next client. A few minutes later, Kim's appointment showed up.

Between up-dos and blow-dries, Kim thought over what Jazzy had said. By the time the workday ended, she'd decided to stop off at her parents' house and see if her mother had time to talk.

Her parents had just sat down to dinner when she arrived. "There's plenty of food," her mother said. "Grab a plate and help yourself."

Kim soon joined her parents with a plate full of her mother's fabulous chicken ziti.

"This is good, Mom," Kim said.

Her mother smiled. "I'm glad you like it. Now what's on your mind?"

Kim cut her eyes over to her dad, who was busy shoveling food into his mouth, clearly oblivious to anything the women were saying. Some things never changed, and this time that was good.

She turned back to her mother. "I'm getting really frustrated about my engagement."

Her mother put down her fork, blotted her lips with her napkin, and leaned toward Kim. "I think that's normal. A lot of brides-to-be have sort of a. . .what do you call it? Buyer's remorse?"

Was that what she had? Maybe, but she didn't think so.

Kim shrugged. "I don't hear from him for days, and I find myself wondering if we really should get married, then I get an e-mail like..." She lifted her hands as her voice trailed off.

"Honey, I'm sure everything will be just fine between the two of you. This separation has been extremely stressful, not only on you, but on David, too, I'm sure."

"Why do you think he proposed before he left, knowing he was about to go?" Kim asked.

Her mother pursed her lips as she thought about it; then she smiled. "David loves you, and he knew he wanted to spend the rest of his life with you. I think he felt that this was the best way of letting you know his intentions."

Kim stood and carried her plate to the sink. "He could have just told me what was on his mind."

"True, but would it have been as powerful as a proposal?"

Her mother had a point. "Probably not."

"There ya go. David doesn't do anything halfway. You'll be glad about that later—after you've been married a few years and have children."

"Maybe." Kim shrugged and turned away.

"Sweetheart." Her mother placed her hand on Kim's shoulder and turned her around. "I wish I could do something to make everything better, but this is something I can't fix. If you love David and still want to marry him, you'll have to wait until he comes back. But if you're having real second thoughts, perhaps you need to rethink your engagement."

A lump formed in Kim's throat as she nodded. "Thanks, Mom. Right now, all I need is a listening ear."

Kim helped her mother clean the kitchen while her dad went to make a business call to California. As they cleared the table, they talked about everything they'd been doing.

Then Kim brought up the get-together at Brian's on Saturday. She noticed that her mother almost dropped the plate she'd been holding.

"Are you okay, Mom?"

"Yes, I'm fine." Her mother put down the plate and cleared

her throat as she turned to face Kim. "I can finish up here. Why don't you go on home and get some rest?"

"But—"

Her dad arrived in the kitchen. "Sorry to interrupt your girl talk, but I need to see your mother," he said to Kim. Then he looked at his wife. "Barb, do you have a few minutes? I need to talk to you about this trip we have planned."

"Trip?" Kim turned to face her parents. "Y'all are going on a trip?"

"We're thinking about it."

"When?" Kim asked.

Her mother looked at her father, who spoke. "That's what I wanted to discuss."

Kim wiped her hands on the dish towel. "Okay, I can take a hint. The two of you want to be alone. Call me tomorrow and tell me more about your trip."

"Okay, honey," her mother replied. "And stop trying to overthink your engagement. David will be home very soon, I'm sure, and you'll wonder why you worried so much."

"Thanks." Kim left her parents' house wondering what had just happened. For the first time in her life, they'd nearly pushed her out the door.

Everyone continued to act strange. Saturday morning, Kim noticed that her schedule ended at noon. Her standing early afternoon appointment had canceled.

"This is odd," she said as she looked over the appointment book. "I'm generally busy all day on Saturday."

Jasmine continued combing her client's hair and didn't look up. "Sometimes it just works out that way. No big deal. Why don't you call it a day and go on home?"

"I can stick around here and help you," she said.

"No." Jasmine stopped what she was doing and looked Kim in the eye. "You have that thing at Brian's place tonight. Go home, take a long bubble bath, and pamper yourself a little. You'll have more fun if you're rested."

Kim chuckled. "It's just a little get-together. Brian has some harebrained notion that he needs to throw a sophisticated party with fancy food. He even wants his guests to dress up."

"All the more reason to do a little primping." She made a shooing gesture. "Now go on; get out of here."

"Okay, okay," Kim said as she swept the last of the hair into the dustpan. "Just promise to call me if you get a walk-in. I really don't mind coming back if you get swamped."

"I'll be just fine," Jasmine said with a self-satisfied smile.

On her way home, Kim's thoughts wandered back over the past several days, and she reflected on how secretive everyone was. And the tension was growing.

It wasn't her birthday, so no one was planning to surprise her. She couldn't think of any reason for people to keep a secret from her.

Kim thought about her parents and how they practically pushed her out the door. They were planning a trip. Without her. It shouldn't have bothered her, but with David out of the country, she felt left out of everyone's lives. No one understood that she needed to be part of something as much as ever.

Maybe her problem was that she was standing still watching the world move forward without her. And as long as David was overseas, she'd be this way. She didn't know what to make of her feelings for Brian. She'd always loved him, but as her romantic thoughts about him increased, she felt like she was sinking deeper into unknown territory—something that frightened her. If she acted on her feelings now, she not only risked hurting David, but she was afraid Brian would freak out.

And then her annoyance annoyed her. When David had proposed, she loved him—or at least she thought she did. But now, as she looked back at the way he'd kept his plans to volunteer for the mission a secret, she wished she'd given him back his ring and told him they'd wait for his return to be officially engaged.

She could still do that, but it meant e-mailing him. Was

that bad form? But then again, he'd proposed without letting her know his plans. What if he did that kind of thing after they said their vows? Could she go through life with someone like that?

By the time she pulled into the driveway, she'd made her decision. She was going to send David an e-mail and tell him she wanted to end—no, make that suspend—their engagement. They could discuss it when he returned.

She heard her phone ringing as she unlocked her door, but it stopped once she was inside. A glance at her caller ID let her know it was Brian.

He must have realized he couldn't pull this thing off without help, she thought with a chuckle. She put her purse down and punched in his number.

"Want me to come help you get ready for this shindig?" she asked.

"Nope. Everything's all set."

"Why did you call?"

Kim heard some whispering in the background. "Who's there?"

"Oh, just someone who stopped by for a little while. Oh, hold on a sec." She heard Brian put his hand over the mouthpiece for a couple of seconds. "Why don't you plan to get here right at seven?"

"That's when it starts. Don't you want me to come help you greet people?"

Brian laughed. "I think I can handle it by myself."

Then it dawned on her. "You have someone else helping out, don't you?"

"You might say that."

"Oh, so there's a mystery woman, huh?" At least something made sense. She forced a smile. "Okay, I'll show up at seven."

"Oh, and Kim, why don't you wear that pearl necklace David gave you for Christmas."

Kim let out a nervous laugh. "Why do you care what jewelry I wear? What's going on, Brian?"

"I just think it's really pretty on you. This is a dress-up party, remember?"

"Okay, whatever. I'll be there," she said, "wearing my pearl necklace if it makes you happy."

"See you at seven. And not a minute before. In fact, it's okay if you're a couple of minutes late."

"Are you sure you still want me to come? I'm thinking you might want to be alone with. . .your new lady."

"There'll be a lot of people here." He snickered. "You'd better come—just not early, though."

Kim changed into a jogging suit and lay down on the couch to watch some TV and rest before getting ready. She'd hung her new black dress on the closet door. She didn't know what she'd been thinking when she let Mrs. Jenner talk her into buying it.

After alternately channel surfing and dozing, Kim finally got up and took the bubble bath Jazzy thought was so important. Then she carefully applied her makeup and got dressed. She looked at the clock on her dresser, and it was only six fifteen. If Brian hadn't told her not to get there early, she would have gone ahead. Now she had to wait.

Time dragged until Kim felt safe to leave and not arrive before seven. As she turned the corner and drove up Brian's street, everything seemed very still. There were a lot of familiar cars parked along the curb, but something seemed strange. Brian's front door was closed, the blinds were pulled, and there was only one window showing a light on in the house.

She felt a gripping sensation. Something was wrong. Kim pulled into his driveway, threw her car into park, turned it off, and hopped out.

Kim ran up the front steps of his small, red-brick house and banged on the door. She needed to be there for him. He'd be so—

"Hello, sweetheart," David said as he opened the door. "Surprised?"

twelve

Kim suddenly froze to her spot on the porch, while David grinned back at her. A group of friends stood in the background, but she was in such a state of shock, all their faces were blurred.

"Hi, honey," David said as he reached for her hand. "Come on in and join the party."

This so wasn't how she wanted to see David when he first came back. "Are you surprised?" Someone shouted from the other side of the room.

"Isn't this exciting?"

"Hey, Kimberly! Looks like we really gotcha this time."

One voice rang out after the other, but all Kim wanted to do was turn around and run. She felt oddly like she was in a bad fairy tale, with all the creepy characters staring at her as she walked through the forest of her nightmare.

David put his arm around her and pulled her close. "You're shaking, Kimberly. Are you cold?"

She opened her mouth, but she still couldn't talk. So she shook her head.

Brian suddenly appeared with a look of concern. "Find her a place to sit, David, and I'll get her something to drink." As he walked away, Kim overheard his voice as he softly told someone, "Maybe surprising Kim wasn't such a good idea."

No kidding.

Having a surprise welcome home party for David would have been awesome. After all, he would have known he was back, and it wouldn't have been such a shock. But this was frightening. Terrifying, in fact. Kim wasn't sure she'd ever get over the jolt of seeing David standing at Brian's door.

Brian arrived with a glass of something with ice in it. "Take a sip of this ginger ale, Kim."

David steadied her hand as she took her first sip. Some of the other people dispersed and talked among themselves, giving her a chance to recover. Finally, Kim felt that she was of sound enough mind to question what had happened.

"How long have you been back?" she asked.

He grinned. "Since last night."

"Here?" Kim shot Brian a glare. "You've been staying with Brian?"

"No," David's mother said as she sneaked up from behind Brian. "He's been with me." Mrs. Jenner gave her a once-over. "That dress looks very nice on you. I was afraid you might not wear the one I picked out."

David's face showed joy. "Is this what you bought when the two of you spent the day together? I love it!"

Kim managed a half smile before looking at Brian as she touched her necklace. "I wore the pearls you asked me to."

David turned her around to face his mother. "These are the pearls I gave her for Christmas."

"They're lovely," Mrs. Jenner said. "Now you need a pearl bracelet to go with it."

"Oh, I don't wear—"

Mrs. Jenner interrupted Kim. "I might have one that matches your necklace."

"She doesn't wear bracelets," Brian said.

"What's wrong with bracelets?" David's mother glared at Brian before turning to Kim. "All girls wear bracelets." She turned to David and patted his arm. "David loves to shower his women with jewelry, don't you, son?"

Kim wondered how many women he'd showered with jewelry. He looked panicked.

"Working in a hair salon makes wearing bracelets difficult for Kimberly," Brian explained. "I'm sure she likes them, don't you?"

She saw his pleading expression, so she nodded. No doubt Brian had the best of intentions when he'd planned this party, and she didn't want to ruin it for him. With that in mind, she made a quick decision.

Kimberly forced the biggest smile she could manage. "I'm sorry I acted like a grump. I was just so surprised to see you, David."

"I knew you would be." His eyebrows lifted as he took her hand and looked into her eyes. "I hope you're as happy as I am."

She swallowed hard and nodded. "Yes, of course I am. Very happy."

Brian tapped Mrs. Jenner on the shoulder and gestured for her to follow him. "Let's leave the happy couple alone for a few minutes so they can catch up."

Once they were alone, David smiled at Kim and gently touched her cheek. "You're as beautiful as ever, Kimberly. I've really missed you."

She felt her heart soften a bit as her fiancé spoke to her with the sweetness she remembered, but she didn't feel that heart-stopping romantic love she so wanted to have. Instead, she found herself wondering what Brian had been thinking. He knew she hated surprises. "Why didn't you tell me you were coming home?"

"I thought a surprise would be more fun."

"Maybe so, but I would have appreciated some warning."

"Why?" he asked. "Would you have done anything different?"

"Probably not, but I wouldn't have felt so lost when you opened the door."

"The look on your face was priceless." He held a lock of her hair between his fingers and twisted it before tucking it behind her ear. That simple, familiar gesture bugged her. "I hope someone got a picture."

Kim pulled her hair away from him and scooted a few inches away from David on the sofa. "They better not have. I don't want pictures of that moment."

David gave her a mock pained look. "It'll be fun to show our grandkids."

That reminded her of one of their earlier conversations,

and she felt a tinge of anger. "We have to have kids to have grandkids, and you said you didn't want kids."

"I've been thinking about it, and I'm not sure yet," he said. "Do we have to discuss this now?"

"There are a lot of things we need to discuss."

Now David's frown was real. "Are you mad at me, Kimberly?"

Some of her anger dissipated, and she shook her head. "No, I'm not mad. But we do need to talk."

"Okay, so talk."

"Not here, David. Not now." She studied his face as he looked her over. "Are you home for good?"

"The first part of the mission is over." He pointed to his leg. "We're not sure if we'll have to go back, but if we do, my part in the plan depends on how quickly I heal."

"What happened to your knee?"

He rubbed it. "That's a long story. I'll tell you about it later. I just hope it's better soon so I can be ready if needed."

"So you're still not sure if you're going back?"

David stroked her hair from her face. "Kimberly, hon, you know there are no guarantees in life." As she started to look down, he cupped her chin and tilted her face toward his. "Let's make the most of the time we have now."

Slowly, she nodded. He was right. There were no guarantees. And *now* was all they had.

&

Brian gripped the tray of drinks as he stood at the door watching David and Kimberly. He sensed the tension between them, and he had to use every ounce of self-restraint to hold back and not see if he could help.

"Don't they look happy?" Kim's mother said as she came up and took a cup from the tray. She stared at him until he looked her in the eye.

"Uh. . .yes, very happy."

Mrs. Shaw blew out a breath of exasperation as she took the tray from him and put it on the breakfast bar. "You know good and well, I was just trying to get your attention, Brian."

He blinked and cocked his head. "What do you mean?"

"My daughter looks absolutely miserable."

Brian licked his lips as he turned back to see what Kim's mother was talking about. David was still talking, and Kim was looking at him, but the chemistry between them seemed off.

"Something's been bothering her lately," Mrs. Shaw continued. "Has she spoken to you about what's on her mind?"

"No, not really," Brian replied. "But I think she's still a little ticked about David not telling her he was planning to volunteer for this special mission in the Middle East."

"Well, I can certainly understand that. I just hope they have a chance to work through some of these issues before they tie the knot."

"Yes, me, too."

Mrs. Shaw lovingly placed her hand on Brian's shoulder and gave him a gentle squeeze. "I know you do. You and Kimberly have been close for so long, you're almost like brother and sister."

He forced a smile. "That's right. Like brother and sister." *Not so much anymore.*

The time seemed to drag for Brian. He thought the party would never end. Finally, all of his guests had thanked him, welcomed David back, and left him alone with what appeared to be a slightly unhappy couple.

"I don't know how to thank you, man," David said as he half-hugged Brian and shook his hand. "It was a bigger success than I ever dreamed."

"Yeah," Brian grunted and cut a glance toward Kim. She cast her eyes downward.

"So is everyone meeting at church tomorrow?" David looked back and forth between Brian and Kim. "I thought we could make plans then."

"Sure, that's fine," Brian said when he realized Kim wasn't helping out.

When she looked at him, he glared at her. She rolled her eyes and smirked.

David reached for Kim's hand. "C'mon, Kimberly, let me walk you to your car." On their way to the door, he looked over his shoulder. "Thanks again, buddy. I owe you big-time."

"No problem."

Brian stood on the porch and waited until they took the last step off his porch before he went inside and closed the door. He left the light on for a few more minutes until he heard Kim's car back out of the driveway. David had parked his car around the corner in the opposite direction from where Kimberly had come.

As he picked up the last of the plates and cups, he felt like kicking himself for contributing to Kim's misery. He didn't know what he'd been thinking when he agreed to spring this surprise on her. Kim hated surprises. Even back in high school when one of her best friends had arranged for a bunch of people to suddenly appear at a little birthday dinner, she'd gotten mad.

&

So it was all a setup. Kim lifted her new dress over her head then carefully hung it on the padded hanger. No wonder everyone had been acting so strange lately. They all knew David was coming home. Jazzy, people from church, David's mom, and even her parents had been there. And to think Brian had been the ringleader. She'd have to let him know what she really thought—but not in front of David. She had a special message for him.

Too bad she wasn't sure what it was yet.

&

Kimberly awoke Sunday morning to the sound of rain pelting her bedroom window. She got up and pulled back the curtain to see how bad the storm was. A bolt of lightning flickered across the sky, followed a few seconds later by a boom of thunder.

Ugh. The weather matched her mood.

After seeing David, there was no doubt she couldn't marry him. The romantic, forever-and-ever kind of love just wasn't there. And what was up with Brian? He should have known better. He'd been with her once before when she was the surprise guest of honor, and she let him know how much she hated it. Maybe he assumed that since David was officially the focus of the get-together, she'd be okay with it.

Kim was sick of thinking about everything. She went about her morning routine of coffee, toast, and a shower. Now, what to wear?

She didn't want to ruin a good pair of shoes in the sloppy mess of the church parking lot, which ruled out half her wardrobe. Finally, after staring at the lineup of clothes, she settled on a gray skirt, a burgundy blouse, and a black sweater. That way she could wear her boots and have a somewhat pulled-together look.

David arrived at her door at precisely the time they'd agreed upon. He held the umbrella as he walked her to the car, held the door, and made sure she was safely inside. He was doing all the right things, but she was still irked.

"You look very pretty this morning," David said. "I thought maybe we could go out after church—just the two of us—and grab a bite to eat."

Of course he never consulted her. She stared straight ahead without a comment.

After a few moments of silence, David touched her arm. "You okay, sweetie?"

She edged away from his touch. "I'm fine."

He blew out an exasperated sigh. "All right, what gives? Why are you acting so testy?"

Kim really didn't want to discuss it now—not before church. But he'd cornered her, and she didn't see that she had a choice. "Why do you always act like I should be happy with all of your decisions?"

"What?" His perplexed expression made her cringe, but she needed to be honest.

"You thought we could go out for a bite to eat after church, but you never asked me what I wanted."

"Well?" he said slowly as he drew his eyebrows together. "Do you want to go out for lunch after church?"

Her shoulders sagged. "Maybe. . .I guess so."

"Something else is going on, I can tell."

Kim squeezed her eyes shut and asked God for help. When she looked at David, she saw his clenched jaw and pulsing temples. He was annoyed, which bothered her even more.

"I'm not happy about the fact that everyone kept your homecoming a secret," she blurted.

"But that was supposed to be a nice surprise."

"A bouquet of flowers is a nice surprise. The musical trio you had at dinner the night we got engaged was a nice surprise. But something as significant as you coming back after not seeing you so long. . ." Her voice trailed off as she tried to think of how to word her thoughts. "It made me feel off-kilter."

He laughed. "Your expression was pretty funny."

Kim shot him a scowl. "It wasn't funny to me. It was humiliating."

David lifted a hand and let it slap back down on the steering wheel. "Okay, I won't do that again. No more surprises—at least not any that will make you feel so—what did you call it? Off-kilter?"

She nodded. Kim knew she should be satisfied, but she still wasn't. And she wouldn't be until she had *that talk* with David. She had to be kind and sensitive, and the timing had to be just right.

They arrived at church a few minutes early, so they were able to get a good seat near their friends. The first thing Kim did was look for Brian. Once she spotted him, she relaxed. Even if she couldn't have him, she liked knowing he was in sight.

David slipped his arm over Kim's shoulder as the pastor began his sermon. And there it stayed until time to sing the next praise song. Kim felt like she was going through the motions of worship, and that made her feel even worse.

After church was over, they went down the hall to the multipurpose room, where David chatted with a few old friends who hadn't been able to make it to his homecoming party. Kim smiled and nodded as everyone told her how happy she must be.

Brian occasionally glanced in her direction and offered a reassuring smile. She felt like he was the only person in the room who really knew her. And after last night, she wasn't even sure about that.

"Would you like something to drink?" David asked. "Coffee?"

Kim started to say no thank you, but when she saw that Brian had gone over to the beverage table, she nodded. "Let me get it, okay? Why don't you stay here and talk to everyone? What would you like?"

David tilted his head and narrowed his eyes. "Are you sure? I don't mind going with you."

"No, I'll do it."

As soon as David told her what he wanted, she took off toward the drinks, leaving him in the midst of a small group. Brian turned as she approached him.

"Feeling better?" he asked before taking a sip of his drink.

"I guess." Kim busied herself, pouring coffee and dumping in the right amount of cream and sugar before turning to face Brian. "Why did you do it?"

Brian cast an apologetic glance her way and shook his head. "I'm really sorry. I should have known better."

"Yes, you should have."

"Forgive me, okay?"

"Fine." She held Brian's gaze for several seconds.

"You better give David the coffee you just fixed, or it'll get cold."

Without another word, Kim picked up the Styrofoam cups and carried them over to where David now stood talking to one man. When she got close enough to listen, she heard him talking about the military.

"Thanks, hon," he said as he gave her a quick glance and took his coffee. Then he turned to the man Kim had only seen once but couldn't remember his name. "I promised my lady some lunch, so we'd better go."

"Great talking to you, David. See you next week?"

"I'll be here," David replied.

As they got to the door closest to the parking lot, Kim saw that the rain had let up, but the pavement was covered with puddles.

"Want me to go get the car and pick you up?" he asked.

"No, that's okay," she replied. "I don't mind walking."

Brian joined them, and they walked out together. Just as she stepped off the sidewalk, onto the road, her foot found a slick spot, and she started to fall.

thirteen

Suddenly she felt David's hand beneath her elbow and Brian's arm around her waist. David quickly moved his hand and pulled her to his side, giving Brian a playful glare.

"I'm back now, buddy. I can take care of my own girl."

Brian's arm lingered at Kim's waist for a couple of seconds before he pulled back. His expression suddenly turned hard.

David hugged Kim to his side. "You okay, hon?"

"Yeah," she said as she continued watching Brian with interest. "I'm fine."

Brian's stern scowl remained as he lifted a hand in a wave. "Gotta run. Glad you're home, David. See you around."

"Let's get you off this slippery parking lot and into the car." David kept his arm around Kim all the way to the car, making it difficult to stay steady without leaning into him.

As soon as Kim was settled in the passenger seat, she lowered her head and silently prayed. *Lord, please be with me and help me handle David's feelings with care.* She kept her eyes closed for a few seconds to reflect on what she needed to do.

"Hey, I thought you were okay. You're not hurting anywhere, are you?" David asked as he clicked his seat belt. Funny, she hadn't heard him get into the car. Her thoughts were still on Brian.

"No, I told you I'm fine. That step down was slick."

"Someone needs to do something about this parking lot. It's treacherous."

And so was the emotional slope she was on, Kim thought.

"What are you in the mood for?" David grinned at her as though they didn't have a care in the world.

She shrugged. "Anything's fine."

"As I recall, you like Chinese food." He turned the key in

the ignition. "I'm in the mood for some moo goo gai pan."

Kim really wasn't in the mood for Chinese food, but if he wanted it, she wasn't about to deny him. "That would be fine." Brian would have known she'd rather have something more traditional after church.

No matter what David talked about, Brian was in the back of Kim's mind. She wondered where he'd run off to or if he was as mad as he looked. Did he have plans for lunch?

"Hey, hon, did you hear what I just said?"

"Uh. . .you want moo goo gai pan?"

David chuckled. "That was at least five minutes ago. I've talked about several things since then."

She turned to him with a sheepish look. "Sorry."

"You're still overwhelmed by the surprise, aren't you, hon?"

"Yes, I must be." All she really wanted now was to go home and think.

"I'm sure a good meal will fix you right up. I was hoping to go for a walk in the park later, but there's no telling what the weather will do."

Kim looked at him, gave him a closed-mouth smile, and nodded. "Nothing much has changed around here."

After they were seated at the restaurant, David leaned toward her, elbows on the table, his gaze fixed on her. "You've always intrigued me, Kimberly."

"Intrigued you?" She lifted an eyebrow.

"Sometimes when I look at you, I can't help but wonder what you're thinking. It's like you have some deep, dark secrets." He paused and reached for her hands across the table. "And I have to admit, that's part of the attraction."

"It is?"

"I like the mystery of the relationship," he admitted. "With some women, I always know what they're thinking. But with you, I'm never sure."

"So you like it when I don't tell you what's on my mind?"

He twisted his mouth and frowned. "That doesn't sound right, does it?"

Kim laughed, in spite of her inner turmoil. "No, it really doesn't."

"Mind if I start over?"

"Go right ahead." She made a sweeping gesture with one hand and tried to pull back the other hand, but he held tight.

He traced the backs of her fingers while she waited to hear what he meant. Finally, he looked into her eyes. "To be honest, I'm not sure what I mean, except you're different from most women."

"Are you trying to tell me something, David?"

After a brief hesitation, he covered her hand with both of his. "Yes, I am. Kimberly Shaw, I'm the most fortunate man alive to have you here waiting for me."

"Thank you." Her stomach ached. This was going to be much more difficult than anything she'd ever done.

"As soon as we're able to, we'll have the biggest and most elaborate wedding of the century."

The very thought of an elaborate wedding made her stomach hurt. In fact, she couldn't even get through the bridal magazine Jazzy had given her. "David, I—"

He lifted one hand and gestured. "I'll hire a skywriter to announce to the world that you and I are finally husband and wife. When we come out of the church, I'll have someone release dozens of birds."

She frowned and shook her head. "I don't think so, David."

"You don't want birds? How about butterflies? I went to a wedding a few years ago, back before I met you, where each of the guests had little cardboard boxes of butterflies. I'll call my buddy and ask him where they found them. We'll release hundreds of butterflies to announce our love for each other."

"David!" She caught herself as the sharpness of her own voice came through.

He tilted his head and looked at her with a pained expression. "You like butterflies, don't you?"

"Yes, of course I do. But that's not what I want."

"Then what do you want, Kimberly?"

"I. . ." Now that she'd been cornered, Kim didn't know what to say or do. She and David had so much to talk about, she didn't know where to begin. And this wasn't the place to do it.

"Would you like something more traditional? Or more of a no-frills wedding?"

She shrugged. "You caught me off guard with this, David. We need to discuss it, but not right now."

He let go of her hands and leaned back in his chair. "You're right. We don't need to be discussing the nitty-gritty details of the wedding until we know when it's gonna be."

Kim's thoughts collided with her emotions. One thing was for certain, though. She couldn't marry David.

"What are you thinking, hon?"

She shook her head. "Not much of anything at the moment."

"Still dumbstruck, huh?"

With a nod, she replied, "Yes, I guess you can say that."

David dug into his moo goo gai pan, while she picked at her chicken fried rice and egg roll. Not only was she not in the mood for Chinese food, but she'd lost her appetite, period.

After David cleaned his plate, he started to stand, but he hesitated. "Ready?"

She nodded and stood, and he led the way to the exit. He paid at the register on the way out, so Kim stood by the door and waited. The one time she'd tried to treat David, his ego had been bruised, so she didn't even bother anymore.

After they got in the car and started toward her house, Kim cleared her throat. "David, you and I really need to talk."

"I know, hon. It's been way too long."

She didn't expect this to be easy, but it appeared to be even more difficult than she thought. "I have to do a few things around the house this afternoon, but can you come back later?"

He glanced at his watch. "I promised Mom I'd help her

with some things, but I don't think it'll take all day."

"Call me when you're done, okay?"

He pulled up in front of her house. She opened the car door before he had a chance to get out. "Kim—"

"I'm perfectly capable of walking to my front door." She gave him a look that she hoped would keep him right where he was. It worked.

Shortly after Kim got home, Brian called. "Will you be home for a while?"

"Yes, but I have to do some laundry."

"Put a load in your washing machine, and I'll be there in fifteen minutes."

Kim started to tell him to wait, but then she remembered that David would probably be over later. "Okay, but I really don't have long."

"I don't need much time," he replied.

Brian arrived five minutes early. Kim had known him long enough to know he'd be early, especially when she heard the sound of urgency in his voice.

"What's so important that can't wait, Brian?" She gestured toward the sofa. "Have a seat?"

"Yeah, but not in there. Let's sit at the table."

Kim shrugged. "Suit yourself." She led the way to the kitchen, where they took seats adjacent to each other. "So what's on your mind, Brian?"

He closed his eyes, lowered his head, and folded his hands in front of him. When he glanced up at Kim, she saw the pain in his eyes. "I can't deal with this whole charade anymore, Kim. I care about you, and I don't like seeing you hurting."

Kim gulped. As much as she wanted to tell Brian everything she'd been thinking, she didn't want to do that until she talked to David. "I care about you, too, Brian, but we've been like brother and sister for so long, I'm not sure you can see things clearly."

"It's different for me," he admitted. "Sure, I used to tease you and treat you like you were a sister. But my feelings—well, I don't know. I'm not sure about them anymore. . . ." His voice trailed off as he looked at her.

"You're not sure?" she whispered.

He blinked and nodded. "I'm not sure when it happened, but I care about you more than—well, more than I should."

"Oh, Brian." Kim's heart fluttered with his words. She shook her head. "I don't know what to say." She wanted to throw her arms around him and profess her undying love.

He leaned forward and narrowed his eyes. "Look me in the eye and tell me how you feel about David."

She blinked. Could it get any harder? "I–I'm engaged to him."

"Do you love him enough to want to spend the rest of your life as his wife?"

Kim lowered her gaze to keep from stumbling. Now that he'd cornered her, she had no choice because she couldn't lie. "No."

Brian flopped back in the chair. "That's what I thought. You don't know how to tell him, do you?"

She gathered her thoughts for a few seconds before looking him in the eye again. "Brian, this is so difficult. How does a person tell someone she can't marry him?"

"So you'd rather follow through with this marriage than do what you feel is right in your heart?"

"No," Kim replied. "But I need to be very careful how I handle things."

Brian's jaw tightened. Kim could see his frustration, and she felt it, too.

"Kimberly," Brian whispered. "I—I really care about you."

"I care about you, too."

"Did you hear me?" he asked.

"Yes, of course I did."

"I don't want to lose you, Kim."

Kim let out a nervous laugh. "You never lost me, Brian. We've always been friends, and that'll never change." Her urge to pull him close nearly won out, so she pushed her chair back to put a few more inches between them.

"You know what I mean." He slowly stood up beside his chair. "I understand what you're going through. Just remember that until the wedding vows are said, it's not too late to change your mind. I like David. He's a good man. Just not the right man for you."

"That's not what you said before," she reminded him.

"I didn't realize it then." Brian shook his head.

"This whole thing feels so—I don't know—strange."

"Look what he's done to you, Kim. He always makes decisions without consulting you. Is that what you want for the rest of your life?"

"No." She held his gaze as they fell silent for a moment.

"Kim." He tilted his head forward and gave her one of his serious looks. "People don't change just because they're married. If anything, it'll get worse."

"Brian. . ." Kim buried her face in her hands. She heard his footsteps as he walked to the door.

"I'll see you around, Kimberly Shaw. You're a wonderful woman. I'm just not sure you trust yourself to go with what you know is right."

Neither of them said good-bye before he walked out the door. Kim didn't even try to stand up right away after he'd gone.

The sound of the washing machine cycle ending prompted Kim to get up. As she moved the clothes to the dryer and re-filled the washing machine, Brian's words reverberated through her mind. *Until the wedding vows are said, it's not too late to change your mind.*

She'd already made her decision. But now that she was aware of the spark between her and Brian, she felt like a traitor.

All afternoon, as she did laundry and tidied up her house, she thought about David, Brian, and her feelings for both of them. She deeply cared for both men, but in different ways. David was strong, smart, and very much a gentleman. Brian was goofy, fun, and someone she could always be herself around—at least until recently. She couldn't think of anything really bad about either guy. In fact, they were both as close to perfect as a human could get, even though they were different.

She'd never forget when Brian first brought David around. He'd prepared her by saying how courageous and patriotic David was. That he was a Christian made him seem even better. He'd come to Christ later in life, but the fact remained, his faith was as strong as anyone's.

She allowed her memories of Brian to take over her conscious thoughts. Over the years, Kim had felt little crushes on Brian. Once when they were in high school, jealous pangs shot through her heart as she listened to him go on and on about how cute one of Kim's friends was. Brian dated the girl a couple of times, and when he quit seeing her, Kim was secretly happy. She told Brian he could do better, so he went in search of someone else. Brian was so charming, he never had to wait long for another girl to latch on to him.

Kim was different. She had dates and even crushes every now and then, but she was never all that enamored of the guys. David was the first man she ever told she loved in a romantic way. She always saw herself only falling for the one man she'd spend the rest of her life with. Brian was the fickle one. For as long as they'd been friends, Brian had fallen in and out of love more times than Kim could count. She knew he'd had romantic thoughts of her at times, but only when she was involved with someone else.

The more she thought about Brian, the more convinced Kim was that he wanted her when she was off-limits in the romance department. But even so, she couldn't marry someone she wasn't sure about.

She made a mental list of things to discuss with David. After she finished all her housework and laundry, he still hadn't called. Finally, she picked up the phone and punched in his cell phone number.

"Hey, hon, I was about to call you. I'm just finishing up something for Mom. I'll be right over."

"Okay, good." She let out a nervous breath. "About how much longer do you think you'll be?"

"Half an hour here, then I thought I'd stop off for a pizza on my way over. Do you have soft drinks?"

She started to say she wasn't in the mood for pizza, but she paused and decided to let it go. "I have tea, lemonade, and a couple cans of soft drinks."

"Okay, good. Any of those will be fine. See you soon, hon."

After she hung up, she went to her room to change into something a little nicer. If it had been Brian, she would have stayed as is.

Stop comparing them! Kim was frustrated with herself for continuing to do that. David and Brian were both wonderful men who loved the Lord.

She settled on a soft, flowing purple floral skirt, a fitted T-shirt that matched some of the flowers, and some ballet flats. David always liked seeing her in a skirt.

An hour passed, and he still hadn't arrived. Kim went to the kitchen and poured herself some lemonade, which she carried out to the living room. She was about to sit down and do a little channel surfing when the doorbell finally rang.

As soon as Kim opened the door, she noticed his wide grin. "I just heard from my commanding officer," he said.

David had arrived empty-handed. "Did you get pizza?" she asked.

He slapped his forehead. "Sorry, I forgot. I was about to call and place my order when I got the call. We can just have one delivered."

After he ordered the pizza, David turned to Kim. "Looks like I might have an opportunity to head back for the next portion of our mission."

"But I thought—"

fourteen

Kim stopped herself before she began an argument. No matter what she did, David was going to continue making decisions without consulting her first. It was clear that he still didn't see her as an equal partner in their relationship, and she felt more justified than ever in her decision.

David reached out and stroked her cheek. "You were saying?"

She reached up and removed his hand. "David, that's what I wanted to talk to you about. I don't think this whole engagement thing is working out."

A flash of pain shot across his face. "What are you talking about, Kimberly? I love you." He folded his arms. "Do you not still love me?"

"I don't know, David. I thought I did." She backed away. "I don't understand why you volunteered to leave again without discussing it with me first. The whole time you were gone, I struggled on so many levels. Doesn't it matter to you what I think—and how I feel?"

"Why didn't you say something before?"

Kim shook her head. "I wanted to." She closed her eyes to gather her thoughts before looking him in the eye.

He narrowed his gaze. "And why didn't you?"

"I felt—I don't know—unpatriotic?"

"Unpatriotic?"

"Yeah. You were doing your duty to protect our country, and I was frustrated because you didn't discuss it with me first. I'm not sure you would have even listened to me anyway."

"C'mon, Kim, you know I can't talk about my mission. It's top secret."

"We're obviously on two different wavelengths. It's not

your mission I wanted to discuss. I wanted you to talk about the *decision* with me and at least listen to how I feel about it."

David snorted. "How you feel?"

"Yes."

"Okay, tell me now. How do you feel?"

Now he was starting to irritate her. "That's not the point, David."

"Oh?" He lifted an eyebrow as he regarded her. "So what *is* the point?"

She raised her hands at her sides then let them drop. "The point is I don't feel that I have any say in anything regarding us. You are deciding to volunteer for these missions without talking to me. You choose where we eat when we go out. You even decided you wanted pizza tonight; and without even asking what I thought, you told me you were bringing it." She gulped back the urge to cry. "And then you forgot. But that's not really the point."

"Why do you get so upset over all this insignificant stuff?" His voice had reached a higher pitch, which made Kim feel even worse.

"It's not insignificant to me."

"I didn't realize that. So tell me what else is bothering you."

"I don't know, David, but that's not all that important right now. I thought that once a couple were engaged, they got together and discussed kids and houses and furniture and china patterns." She paused for a couple of seconds before adding, "And jobs."

"Oh, Kim, honey," he said as he reached for her and pulled her to his chest. "I never wanted to make you feel that I don't pay enough attention to you."

Don't cry, don't cry. She bit down on her lip to redirect the pain and keep a tear from falling.

David stroked her back a few times then held her at arm's length. "What if I promise to be more attentive? Would that make you happy?"

"It would have before." Kim hung her head then slowly

raised it and looked him in the eye. "David, I don't think we should stay engaged."

"Shh." He reached over and gently touched her lips. "I know I've hurt you. I love you. I'll try to do better."

"But—" Kim's chest ached. "It's not that—"

"Being a fiancé doesn't come naturally to me," he admitted. "Someone should teach a class on how an engaged man should act." He grinned and tweaked her chin. "Why don't we talk about everything tonight and get it all out? That's the best way we can settle any problems before they get out of hand."

She opened her mouth, but nothing came out. Breaking her engagement with an insensitive man would have been much easier. This surprise show of tenderness had caught her off guard.

The pizza arrived a few minutes later. David paid for it while Kim went to the kitchen to get their drinks. They sat down at the kitchen table.

David took her hand closest to him. "I'll say the blessing—unless you'd rather do it."

She shook her head. "No, that's okay. You can do it."

As they ate, David explained as much as he was able to about his mission—when he'd leave again and when he expected to be back home. He asked if she wanted him to call his commanding officer to see if it was too late to back out. "I've told you already how much I love you, Kimberly. I don't want to risk losing the best thing that's ever happened to me."

Her heart felt like it would pound right out of her chest. "You don't need to do that. There's a much bigger world out there besides what's going on with me."

David leaned forward on his elbow. "I just want to make sure you know how important you are to me. I want you to be happy. I'll do anything to please you, Kimberly, because I love you so much."

His willingness to do whatever it took to make her happy stunned her. She should have been over-the-moon thrilled. How could she break the engagement after what he'd just said?

After he left, Kim twirled the engagement ring on her finger, something she found herself doing when she was deep in thought about anything related to David. It still bothered her that she had to tell him things any intelligent man should have known.

❧

When Brian's cell phone rang, he jumped. He glanced down and saw David's number, so he flipped it open and answered.

"Hey, Brian. Man, I had a close call tonight."

"Oh yeah? What happened?" Brian put down his book and repositioned himself in the chair.

"Kim let me have it."

"What did she let you have?"

"You know," David said, chuckling. "She read me the riot act about what a lousy fiancé I've been."

"Why don't you start from the beginning and explain?"

David cleared his throat before giving Brian a play-by-play accounting of his conversation with Kim. "Who knew she was so sensitive? I never saw that in her before."

"She's not any more sensitive than anyone else would be in her situation." Brian had to work hard not to blast David for his lack of understanding.

"I don't know, man. She obviously doesn't get how the military works."

Brian bristled. "Have you thought about explaining it to her?" Anger bubbled in Brian's chest, but he used every ounce of self-restraint to tamp it down. He needed to keep his head straight for Kim.

"Yeah, maybe I should."

"I think so." Brian dug deep to find the right words to say—for Kimberly. "I know you're the one putting your life on the line for our country, but you need to remember that it's not easy on Kim, not knowing where you are or when you're coming home."

"Point taken."

Finally, he couldn't take it anymore. He had to know. "Did

the two of you work things out?"

David chuckled. "Yes, of course we did. You don't think I'm a fool, do you?"

"No, I never thought that."

"The last thing I need to do is have Kim mad at me when I take off again," David continued. "I love her, and I want to marry her as soon as I return."

Whoa. "Back up, David. You're leaving again?"

"Yes, that's the next thing I wanted to tell you. I'm being deployed in two weeks. You did such a nice job of looking after Kimberly, I wanted to thank you and ask you to do it again. Maybe you can remind her how much I love her when she's unhappy."

"I don't need someone to tell me to look after Kim. First of all, she's perfectly capable of taking care of herself. And second—"

"Okay, okay, I hear ya. I just don't want some other guy coming in and sweeping her off her feet."

"Kim is trustworthy." Even if he couldn't have her, he'd defend her honor to the end.

"I know she is, Brian." David let a couple of seconds pass before he continued. "In the meantime, I think we all need to get together as much as possible before I leave. It'll give me some memories to reflect on when I'm in the trenches."

"Just say when," Brian said as he continued to hold back his temper. "I'll be there." *For Kim.*

Brian couldn't help the fact that he resented David more as each day passed.

❧

Kim got to work five minutes early the next morning, but Jasmine had already arrived. The shop was open and ready for customers.

"Enjoying having David home?" Jasmine asked.

Kimberly nodded and looked away. "Of course."

Jasmine regarded Kim with suspicion. "Really, Kimberly?"

"Yes." Kim heard the frustration in her own voice.

"Oh, sweetie, what's wrong?"

This was one time Kim wished she'd waited a few minutes and come in late. Oh well. She figured she might as well fess up, or she'd have to pretend all day.

"David told me he's going back on another mission."

"You're kidding." Jasmine shook her head and made a henlike clucking sound. "What is that boy thinking?"

"He's a dutiful military man."

Jasmine cast a you've-got-to-be-kidding look her way. "There's dutiful, and there's obsessed. I'd say he's about to cross that line if he hasn't already. Did he discuss it with you first?"

"Well, sort of."

"Sort of?" Jasmine asked.

"Not exactly. He was asked if he wanted to put in for the assignment, and he accepted. But when I told him how I felt—"

"You told him?"

Kim nodded. "Yes, and he was surprised by my reaction."

"Good for you, Kimberly! I'm proud of you." Jasmine beamed. "So what did he say when you told her your feelings?"

"He said it probably wasn't too late to talk to his commanding officer. But I could tell he really wanted to go."

"Don't tell me you said it was okay."

Kim's shoulders sagged. "Jazzy, what could I do when he reminded me that he's in the military to protect our country? It makes me feel like such a slacker for whining about my feelings."

"No, you are not a slacker, Kimberly Shaw. You're just a woman who wants her man around so you can get on with your life."

"But he has this really important job, and I knew how much his military career meant to him when I first agreed to be his wife."

"That doesn't mean you have to let this continue." Jasmine widened her stance and planted her hands on her hips. "Have you discussed this with Brian?"

Kim shuddered as she remembered her conversation with Brian and the unspoken words that still lingered in her thoughts. "No, but I'm sure he probably already knows."

"Don't make a mistake with your life just because you thought you knew what you wanted before you had all the facts."

"I'll try not to," Kim said, just to end the conversation. She had to change the subject. "Have you seen the latest flatiron? That thing's amazing. It can straighten a whole head of ringlets in minutes."

Jasmine offered an understanding smile. "There are a lot of things we need to straighten out, Kimberly. Too bad the latest and greatest flatiron can't fix everything."

Kim laughed. "You got that right."

"Oh, your first appointment canceled. There was a message on voice mail when I got in."

Relieved, Kim went to the storage room and pulled out what she needed for her next appointment. After she got everything organized at her station, she went to the break room with her cell phone and called Brian.

"You're not gonna believe what happened," she said as soon as he answered his phone.

"David called me." Brian sounded angry. "He said you weren't happy about it."

"That's putting it mildly. But we talked it out, and I think he understands how I feel now."

"But it doesn't change anything, does it, Kim?"

She thought for a moment before replying, "No, I guess it doesn't. He's still going, but I told him I was okay with it."

"Are you, Kim?" Brian asked with a sarcastic tone. "Do you know what you want?"

"I have no idea how to answer that. Please don't make this harder than it already is."

He audibly exhaled. "So why did you call me?"

"I just wanted to make sure you knew he was leaving again."

"Does this mean I have to have another party when he comes back?" Sarcasm was evident in his voice.

"Only if you tell me first."

"Trust me, I will," he said. "I learned my lesson."

"David mentioned something about everyone getting together before he leaves. Got any ideas?"

"Why should I have ideas for David? If he wants to get together, he can organize it himself."

"I'm sorry, Brian. It's just that—"

"Don't worry about it," he said, interrupting her. "What do you think about bowling and pizza one night?" His monotone let her know he'd put his emotions on the back burner for her. Again.

The line grew silent for a second. "Brian?"

"Yes, Kim?"

"Thank you."

He laughed. "Why are you thanking me?"

"For being there," she said softly. "For being my friend."

❧

After they hung up, Brian stared at the phone. Even though he felt a kick in the gut every time he saw her with David, she'd always brought light into his life by being there when he really needed her, even when he didn't deserve it. He couldn't let her down, no matter how he felt about her.

In the afternoon meeting, Jack gave him a thumbs-up for his presentation. At least something was going his way.

That night David called. Brian told him the same thing he'd said to Kim about things the group would enjoy.

"Sounds good," David agreed. "How about bowling this Friday night?"

"Fine. I'll e-mail everyone."

"Thanks, buddy. See you then."

After he got off the phone, Brian sat back and thought about hanging out with Kim and David. He knew it wouldn't be easy, but he wasn't about to disappoint Kim.

She called him on Tuesday just to chat. When he said he

was too busy to talk and cut their conversation short, she sounded hurt, but she said she understood.

On Wednesday, Brian felt bad, so he called her and asked if she was okay. She was slow to respond, but after he prodded her with a couple of teasing comments, she chuckled. The sound of her laughter warmed him from the inside out. He'd settle for any kind of relationship he could have with Kim—just to be in her life.

"I've contacted everyone about getting together Friday night," he said. "Too bad about the circumstances, though."

After they got off the phone, Brian prayed. *Lord, give me the strength to handle the inevitable with Kimberly. You know what is right for both of us, so if I can't be the love of her life, help me to be a better friend.* He opened his eyes for a few seconds before shutting them again. *And I pray that these romantic feelings I have for her will subside.*

Thursday and Friday seemed to crawl by, but finally Friday night arrived. After work he went home and changed into some bowling clothes. Everyone was supposed to meet at Graziano's for pizza; then they'd all head over to the bowling alley.

Brian was the first to arrive, so he secured a couple of tables next to each other. People from their singles group trickled in—some in pairs and others alone. The last to arrive were David and Kimberly. All heads turned when they entered.

As people tossed jokes and comments about David taking off again, Brian sat and tried hard not to stare at Kim. However, he did allow himself a glance every now and then, and he could tell she wasn't happy—even behind that plastic smile frozen on her face.

When the pizzas arrived, Brian forced himself to eat. But when he looked in Kim's direction again, he saw that she'd barely nibbled the one piece on her plate. David, on the other hand, was reaching for his third slice, talking with Jonathan on the other side of him and acting as if he didn't have a care in the world.

Brian was about to speak to Kim, but David leaned over in her direction and pointed to something behind Brian. *Must be nice to have someone to whisper to—especially if that person was Kim.* He worked at averting his gaze, but David stood up and tapped his fork on the side of his glass.

David lifted his hand, cleared his throat, and looked directly at Brian. "Now that everyone's here, we can finish dinner and head on over to the bowling alley."

Brian glanced over his shoulder and saw a very tall, very blond, very made-up woman smiling back at David. He'd never seen her before in his life.

fifteen

Kim glanced up to see what David was gesturing toward. An unfamiliar woman stood at the door, looking dazed, but when she noticed David, she smiled and took a step toward their group.

"Do you know her?" she whispered to David.

"Yes, this is Mercedes, my commanding officer's niece. I figured that since she was visiting and didn't have anything to do, she might want to join us." He patted the chair next to him. "Have a seat, Mercedes."

As soon as Mercedes sat, the murmur of the group came to a grinding halt, and the silence grew very uncomfortable. Kim's next reaction was to look at Brian, who hung his head.

"Brian," David said loud enough for everyone at both tables to hear. "This is Mercedes." He turned to the woman. "Mercedes, this is the guy I told you about."

Kim was surprised that Mercedes' already-wide smile got even bigger as she stood, leaned across the table, and extended her hand. Brian stood and shook hands then waited for Mercedes to sit back down.

"Nice to meet you," he muttered through an awkward smile.

David leaned toward Kim and whispered, "I thought they might like each other. Looks like I was right."

Suddenly an odd sensation coursed through Kim. Although she knew David had invited a guest, she had no idea he wanted to fix Brian up. She wanted to shake David until his teeth fell out for making her look involved in his scheme. From the look on Brian's face, she knew he wasn't any happier about it than she was.

"Let's go, folks," David said as he stood. "I'm feeling a few strikes coming on."

As they left the restaurant, Kim fell back from the group, and Brian made his way to Kim's side. "Why didn't you warn me?" he asked without looking her in the eye.

"I had no idea. I'm really sorry, Brian."

"Yeah, I bet." His tone left no doubt that he didn't believe her. With all these people around, she couldn't grovel and beg for his forgiveness.

"Hey, hon!" David called out. "You coming?"

Kim gave Brian an apologetic look then ran to catch up with David. "I don't think this was such a good idea."

He gave her a what's-your-problem look. "They'll be fine after they get to know each other."

"Did you see his face?" Kim shook her head. "He's mad."

"Better mad than sad. I don't like my buddy being lonely. He needs a pretty girl to talk to." David put his arm around Kim and gave her a squeeze. "I think he might even be jealous that I have you."

Kim's breath caught in her chest. "I don't think he's jealous of you."

"Maybe not, but I still think it'll do him some good to get out and date a little."

Kim glanced over her shoulder in time to see Mercedes and Brian talking as they walked toward the row of cars at the edge of the parking lot. Brian looked up at her, so she snapped her attention back to David.

"See?" David said. "They're hitting it off just fine. Now we won't have to worry about him."

Kim thought for a moment. "I guess you're probably right." An overwhelming sadness filled her, but she tried not to let on. She knew Mercedes wasn't Brian's type, so she didn't feel jealous. It just bugged her that he was angry, thinking she knew about David's plan.

All the way to the bowling alley, David talked about how Mercedes and Brian would be a great match because she was so pretty and fun to be around. Kim half listened as she thought about all the reasons Brian and Mercedes *wouldn't* be a good match. Brian was an outdoorsy kind of guy, and she looked like a high-maintenance girl. Brian had moods, but all this girl did was smile. Brian liked—

The sudden realization smacked Kim so hard, she nearly fell over. Kim now had no doubt that she couldn't marry David. She couldn't discuss it now, but she wouldn't wait much longer.

"What's wrong, hon?" He gently jostled her.

Kim had to come up with something quickly. "Do you know where she is spiritually?" she asked David. "Is she a Christian?"

David shrugged. "I would assume so. Her uncle and parents go to church."

"That doesn't make her a Christian." She thought for a moment as she realized what he'd just said. "You know her parents?"

He nodded. "Her dad retired shortly after I met her uncle. I went to his retirement party."

Kim sat back and pondered her next question before asking. "Does she like sports?"

"Why are you asking me? We'll be at the bowling alley soon, and you can talk to her. I think it would be nice for you to get to know each other—especially since she and Brian seem to be hitting it off."

Once they got inside the bowling alley and she took one good look at Brian's face, she wanted to talk to Brian. He looked absolutely miserable, while Mercedes stood there jabbering away.

David arranged for the four of them—Brian, Mercedes, Kim, and himself—to be on a lane together. He nudged Kim and whispered, "That way we can keep an eye on them and make sure everything goes well."

"We can't force them," Kim argued.

"No, but we can toss out some conversation starters."

Throughout the first game, Kim watched David try his hardest to engage Brian, but all he got was a sulky demeanor and a few grunts every now and then.

Most of the group agreed that they were having too much fun to stop after the first game, so they decided to bowl another one. Brian didn't say anything, but he didn't leave.

"I need a little break," David said as he motioned for Kim to follow him. "We'll be right back, folks," he told the others. "I need to talk with my fiancée for a minute."

"I don't get it," David said as soon as they were out of hearing distance. "He's not even trying. That's not like Brian."

It was very much like Brian. Over the years that Kim had known him, she'd learned to sense when to back off, and that time had come more than an hour ago.

"Let's just back off for now, okay?" she asked. "Don't try so hard. Brian has a mind of his own."

David lifted his eyebrows and shook his head. "I give up. I can't make Brian happy."

"No, you really can't," Kim agreed. She leaned over and nodded her head toward the lanes. "Let's go back with the others."

After David quit trying so hard with Brian and Mercedes, Kim felt a sense of relief. Brian relaxed a little, too.

Mercedes wasn't as interested in bowling as she was in David's stories about military life. "I've always enjoyed listening to my uncle and dad talk about the military." She tilted her head and grinned at David. "Did you always know you wanted to be in the National Guard?"

"No," he replied. "When I was younger, I thought I'd go into the army, but when I met Colonel Anderson, my thinking went in a whole new direction." He snickered. "Then there was my dad urging me to follow him into his law practice."

"Are you talking about Colonel Harley Anderson?"

"That's the man," David said with a grin and a quick nod. "How did you know?"

Her eyes lit up. "He and my dad used to play golf together."

"Oh yeah," David said with a chuckle. "I heard about that. Your dad was a decent golfer back in his day—at least according to your uncle."

Mercedes tossed her blond hair over her shoulder and laughed. "Better not tell him that. He thinks he's still all that on the golf course."

"Maybe I should challenge him to a game one of these days."

Kim sat back and watched as Mercedes continued giving all her attention to David. "That would be great. Ever since he retired, he's been moping around and acting like there's nothing left to live for—that is, except when he can find someone to play golf with."

"Everyone needs something to motivate them," Kim said.

David let his glance graze her before turning to face Mercedes again. "Kim's right. If golf is what gets your dad out of the house, I need to give him a call before I leave."

Kim cast a glance toward Brian, who gave her an odd look. Kim felt uneasy as she watched the chemistry between David and Mercedes.

Mercedes bounced around in her chair. "I can't wait to tell Dad about you."

Kim felt as though she and Brian were invisible. This whole outing had turned into a David and Mercedes event.

What made it so weird was that she really didn't even care about David turning his back on her to talk to Mercedes. What bothered her was how it made Brian feel. As the evening wore on, Brian got grouchier and more agitated.

Finally, after he bowled his last frame, Brian stood and faced David. "It's been fun, folks, but I need to run." He lifted his eyebrows as he turned toward Mercedes. "I'll take you back to your car now."

David snapped his fingers. "Oh, that's right. I forgot some of us carpooled over here. Too bad."

Brian stood nearby waiting. Kim felt an emotional tug, but she wasn't sure what to do.

"Would you like for us to take you to your car, Mercedes?" David asked.

"Oh," she said, "I wouldn't want to impose."

"We don't mind, do we, Kim?" David asked.

Before Kim had a chance to say a word, Brian stepped up. "I want to take her. The two of you need more time together, since you'll be going back to the Middle East soon." Brian glared at David, almost in a dare.

Kim held her breath as she realized that Brian was coming to her rescue. She felt pulled toward her childhood friend, but David reached for her hand and held it between his. "You're right, Brian. Besides, I think it would be great for you and Mercedes to spend a little more time together." He glanced at Kim and winked before looking back at Brian. "Get to know each other better."

Once they turned in their bowling shoes and everyone else was out of hearing distance, Kim touched David on the arm. "David, we need to talk. Now."

He stopped tying his shoes as he looked up at her. "Sure, hon. Wanna talk here or go somewhere quiet?"

"Somewhere quiet would be nice."

"I know just the place."

There he goes again, she thought. "Why don't we just go to my house?" she said.

"I was thinking—"

"We'll go to my house."

He lifted an eyebrow as he regarded her with interest. "Well, okay then. Your house it is."

As soon as they got to her place, David closed the door and stood facing her. "I assume you want to set the date."

"David, I—uh. . ."

"Hey, hon, I understand. I feel awful about keeping you on hold like I have. Would it help to get it all nailed down tonight?" He took a step toward her and started to put his arms around her.

"No," she said as she backed away. "That's not what I want."

He put his hands in his pockets. "You don't want me to hold you?"

"I don't want to set the date," she replied. "And I don't want to marry you."

Kim worked the ring off her finger and tried to hand it to David. He shook his head.

"I don't think you need to react so strongly," he said. "She was flirting with me, not the other way around."

"What are you talking about?"

"Mercedes." He rubbed the back of his neck and chuckled. "I had no idea you were jealous of Mercedes and me."

"I am not jealous of you and Mercedes!"

"Then what's your problem?" he asked, glancing down at the ring. "What's this all about?"

"I already told you. I don't want to marry you."

"But why? I thought you loved me."

"I did," she said then corrected herself. "At least I thought I did. But after you left, I had some time to myself to think about things—to think about us."

"Is there someone else in your life?"

Kim didn't want to let on how she felt about Brian. But she didn't see any way around it, since he'd find out soon anyway. Lies were never good.

"David, I feel really bad about this, but after you left, Brian did what you asked him to do, and he made sure I wasn't lonely."

"Did he introduce you to someone else?" David said.

"Why would he do that?"

With a shrug, David replied, "He's been your best friend for a long time, and he doesn't want you to be lonely. Don't think I haven't noticed the way he glares at me."

"No," Kim said slowly. "He didn't introduce me to someone else." She closed her eyes for a few seconds then looked directly at David. "This is hard for me to tell you, but I think it's only fair to be the one to say it. I'm in love with Brian."

David's eyes popped wide open in complete shock. "You're what?"

"I know. Brian and I have been such good friends for so long, it almost seemed wrong."

"So my best buddy has been making the moves on my girl when I turn my back. I never saw this one coming."

"No. That's not true. He never made any moves on me."

David's handsome face suddenly turned to a scowl. "You do realize that he's on the rebound after what Leila did. I can't believe you haven't figured that out."

She didn't feel like arguing about Brian's feelings or defending herself or Brian. Instead, she went on the offense. "It doesn't matter. Even if Brian doesn't feel like I feel, I can't marry you."

"This is a huge mistake, Kimberly. You and I are great together."

"I don't think so. I would have become frustrated, and you would have eventually gotten bored with me."

"That never would have happened." He actually smiled for a split second. "I'm a good provider, and you're a sweet Christian woman who would make a wonderful wife."

"How do you know that's what I want?"

"I thought you did."

"I want more, David. I want to know that the man I'm married to considers me an equal partner in big decisions. I want to be consulted before my husband decides to volunteer for dangerous military assignments."

"You should have told me this before I left. Why didn't you say something?"

"I never had the opportunity."

David stared down at the floor as they grew silent. When he looked back into her eyes, she saw that he'd resigned himself to accepting her decision without further argument.

"Are you okay?" she asked.

"Yes, I'm fine. I just have a little self-examination to do."

"David, I think you're a great guy. I have no doubt you'll make some woman a wonderful husband. But not me."

"Okay. I guess I need to leave now."

She stood at the door and waited until he got in his car and drove away. Then she closed the door and leaned against it with her eyes closed.

Lord, I pray that Your will be done in David's and my lives.

❧

She what?" When Brian saw David's number on his caller ID the next day, he assumed it was to find out how things went with Mercedes, not this.

"You heard me, buddy," David said. "I just got the kiss-off because she's in love with you."

sixteen

Brian was so astounded he didn't know what to say. All h[e]
managed was a grunt.

"So what did you do when I was away, man? I asked you t[o]
watch after her, not betray me."

Suddenly fury rose inside Brian. "Trust me, David, I didn['t]
betray you."

"Then what did you say to make her break off ou[r]
engagement?"

"We don't need to discuss this over the phone. If you wan[t]
to talk about it, let's do it face-to-face."

"Fine," David snapped. "Name the place and time, and I'[ll]
be there."

This suddenly felt like a duel. "How about the church afte[r]
I get off work?"

David snickered. "So now you wanna hide behind you[r]
piety?"

Brian tamped back the anger that felt as though it migh[t]
blow through the top of his head. "No, I just want to mak[e]
sure we don't forget our faith." And it didn't hurt that th[e]
pastor would be nearby if they needed him.

"That's okay with me. It doesn't matter where we mee[t]
because I know I've been faithful to the woman I love, eve[n]
though my best buddy was working his way into her heart."

"We'll discuss that this afternoon," Brian said in th[e]
calmest voice he could manage.

After he hung up, Brian bowed his head and prayed fo[r]
mercy for his anger, such terrible thoughts about David, an[d]
guidance in how to talk to him. This was by far one of th[e]
most difficult things he'd ever had to do.

Jack waved as he passed Brian's open door. He'd barel[y]

gotten a couple of steps away before he backed up.

"Whoa, why the wild look?"

Brian relaxed his face and rubbed his neck. "It's complicated."

"Wanna talk about it?"

Brian thought about it then shook his head. "I don't think so. I need to finish balancing this. . ." He held up a stack of pages. "And it looks like it might take me the rest of the day. I can't stay late tonight."

"Got a date?" Jack asked.

"Not exactly. We can talk some other time, okay?"

Jack held up both hands. "Fine, I can tell when I'm being dismissed. Just don't let whatever it is get to you so bad. They're not worth it."

"Who's not worth it?"

Jack smirked and shook his head. "C'mon, Brian. You know what I'm sayin'."

"Thanks for the advice," Brian said with a forced smile. "Would you mind closing the door on your way out?"

After he was alone, Brian called the pastor and asked if he could stick around a few minutes late. Then he managed to shut everything out while he finished his work. Kim called, but Brian told her he was too busy to talk.

She sounded hurt, but this was one day he couldn't stay even five minutes late, and he didn't need to talk to Kim just yet. Since David was the first to tell him about the breakup, he thought it would be best to hear his side first. Kim would understand later.

At five thirty, Brian took off toward the parking lot, practically running so no one would stop him. He was relieved when he got to his car without so much as a good-bye from anyone.

All the way to the church, Brian prayed to keep his mind focused on the mission of working through things and clarifying his intentions. He didn't need to express everything he thought with David. Pastor Jeremy Rawlings motioned him into his office as he walked through the side door.

"What's going on?" Pastor Rawlings asked.

Brian gave him a quick rundown of the phone call. He tried to keep his tone neutral.

"You're not worried, are you?"

"Just a little—for Kimberly's sake, anyway."

Pastor Rawlings offered a sympathetic nod. "I can certainly understand why. I'll stick around until I hear from you."

"Thanks, Pastor."

The sound of a car pulling into the driveway caught their attention. "Why don't you go on into the adult Bible classroom, and I'll let him know where he can find you."

"Great idea," Brian said as he turned and headed off in the direction of the classroom wing.

Three minutes later, David's shadow darkened the doorway. "We have some serious issues to discuss, buddy."

"Come on in." Brian patted the table. "Why don't we sit across the table from each other so we can really talk?" He'd set up folding chairs and put a couple of Bibles on the table in case they needed them.

As soon as they were situated, Brian leaned back and looked David in the eye. "Why don't you start at the beginning and tell me what happened?"

David folded his arms and narrowed his eyes before shaking his head. "First, you tell me what's been going on between you and Kimberly."

"Nothing that hasn't been going on for the past fifteen years," Brian replied.

"Something had to happen for her to suddenly think she's in love with you."

Brian's mind spun with all sorts of possibilities, but he worked hard to maintain his composure. "Did she actually come right out and say that?"

"Yes."

That sure did complicate things. Brian wondered why Kimberly told David before cluing him in—that is, if she really did.

"And you don't think you assumed this, based on something else she said?"

"Look, buddy, I don't assume things. I know what I heard. She flat-out said, 'I'm in love with Brian.'"

If he'd heard this news at any other time from anyone else, Brian would have jumped out of the chair, kicked up his heels, and shouted his joy from the mountaintops. However, joy wasn't what he felt at the moment. He wanted to comfort his friend and at the same time process this new information. But he couldn't do either.

"Want me to talk to her?" Brian asked.

David let out a sinister snicker. "Yeah, so you can laugh at me behind my back? No thanks." He pounded the table hard enough to send an echo through the room. "I can't believe I've been such a big sucker, believing in my girl and my best friend. I trusted both of you."

Pastor Rawlings appeared at the door. "You two okay?"

Brian nodded. "We're fine."

David stood. "Looks like we're done here. I have nothing else to discuss."

"Would you like to give me a chance to tell you my side of this?" Brian asked.

"So you admit there is something going on?"

"No," Brian replied. "Don't put words in my mouth."

"Then tell me your side."

"Before you left, you asked me to watch after Kimberly. I found out from her that you told her to look after me, since I'd just been jilted at the altar."

"Looks like the two of you did your jobs, then," David said with a sneer. "Both of you are a couple of two-timers, and that's all there is to it. Neither of you can be trusted." He glanced over at Pastor Rawlings. "And you call yourselves Christians."

"We didn't need you to tell us to be friends," Brian said as he stood to face David. He wasn't going to let David steamroll him, but more than that, he wasn't about to let

David get away with what he was saying about Kimberl
"She and I have always been there for each other, and yo
know that. Kim is one of the most committed Christians I'v
ever met." He tilted his head forward and glared at David
"And loyal to a fault."

"Not from where I stand."

"What would you have wanted her to do, then, David
Should she have just stayed engaged to you, even though sh
didn't want to be your wife?"

"Well—no, but I would have thought—"

"I think you know as well as I do that neither Kimberl
nor I would have done anything behind your back."

"Right," David said with a sarcastic snicker.

Brian was glad the pastor was still there, he was so angr
"Do you realize what you've done to Kimberly?"

David narrowed his eyes. "What I've done to her? He
buddy, you're getting this whole thing all twisted."

"No, you're the one who's twisting things. You started ou
making her feel like she was the most important person in
your life, and that made her very happy. She fell in love with
the David who treated her with kindness and respect. Then
after the engagement, I watched as you slowly pushed her ou
of your inner circle."

"That's ridiculous. I don't even know what you're talking
about. Inner circle?"

Brian had to pause to keep his temper in check. "After yo
got engaged, Kimberly never knew where she stood with you
When you came to her and announced that you'd volunteered
for this special mission, she was hurt that you didn't consul
her first, but she accepted it. The whole time you were over
there, she worried about you. For all she knew, you could
have been blown to bits by a suicide bomber."

David rolled his eyes. "Aren't you being rather melodramatic
now, buddy?"

"When you came home, she had to fall in line with everything you wanted—from the party to the places you went."

"Did she tell you all this?" David asked.

"I already told you, I figured it out on my own. Kimberly and I have known each other long enough, we can almost read each other's thoughts."

As Brian talked, he noticed a gradual change in David's demeanor—from combative to remorseful. Brian figured he'd said enough.

David glanced over at the door, so Brian looked up. The pastor was no longer there.

After a long, uncomfortable minute, David turned back to Brian. "Look, man, this was a shock. I had no idea Kimberly wasn't still madly in love with me."

"Same here," Brian said as he held up his hands. "All I knew was that she was hurting."

"Give me some time to think through this, okay?" David pursed his lips and waited.

"Sure, that's reasonable." Brian was relieved.

"I'll talk to you again before I take off for my next assignment."

"That'll be good."

After David left, Brian bowed his head and gave thanks that only words had been exchanged. When he looked up again, Pastor Rawlings was back.

"Wanna talk?" the pastor asked.

Brian didn't want to talk, but he felt that he owed the pastor an explanation. "It's complex."

"I bet it's nothing I haven't heard before."

"Maybe so, but this is the first time anything like this has happened to me."

"Let's go to my office where we can be more comfortable."

Brian followed Pastor Rawlings out the door, down the hall, and into the wood-paneled office. As soon as the pastor sat in the overstuffed chair, Brian positioned himself on the sofa on the other side of the table.

"So what's up?" Pastor Rawlings said. "Obviously woman trouble."

Brian nodded. "In the worst kind of way. It's a long story."

The pastor nodded. "Jennifer is staying with her sister for a few days, helping with the new baby, so I have all the time you need."

Brian started slowly from the beginning, about how he and Kimberly had met and become fast friends in elementary school. He talked about how he'd had a huge crush on her off and on since their early teen years, but he never felt he stood a chance, so he settled into remaining her buddy and confidant.

"Did you ever open up to her and see how she felt?" the pastor asked.

"I started to a couple of times, but I always chickened out."

The pastor laughed. "Some men struggle with communication. Perhaps we should take lessons from women who love to talk."

"I kept hoping she'd say something—you know, give me some kind of hint that she might consider me more than just a good guy friend."

Pastor Rawlings leaned forward and listened with all his attention as Brian spilled everything that had been on his heart for the past fifteen years. Finally, Brian shook his head.

The pastor leaned back and rubbed his chin. "Seems I recall you're the one who brought David to church and introduced him to Kimberly."

Brian snickered. "Yup, that was me, chump of the year. I thought they'd hit it off, but I had no idea what David had up his sleeve. I didn't even have a chance to tell him how I felt about her."

"Why didn't you say something before you introduced them?"

"I didn't think it was an issue." Brian shrugged. "Then I had to go away for the National Guard a few weeks during the summer. He'd changed units, so we went at different times, and when I came back, they were tight."

"Yeah," the pastor said as he nodded in understanding, "I

can see how that would pose a problem."

"My timing has been off with Kimberly since I met her. The one other time I thought I stood a chance with her, I waited a couple of weeks to say anything. That was back in high school. Some new guy came along, and next thing I knew, she was swooning over him—just like the rest of the girls. I listened to her go on and on about how great he was, and next thing I knew, they were together."

The pastor laughed. "How long did that last?"

"About half our junior year. Then one thing after another happened. . . ." Brian held out his hands. "And now this."

"This is different for you, huh?"

"Very different," Brian agreed as he reflected on how he'd almost shared his feelings with Kim. "I just don't understand why she told David how she felt about me before she said something to me."

"Well, she was engaged to David," the pastor said. "I agree it would have been better to break it off with him without telling him she loved you, and then come and let you know how she felt. I'm sure it was just an honest error in judgment."

"I always thought Kimberly was one to speak her mind," Brian said. "Back when we were kids, she was able to keep other people's secrets, but she's never been good at hiding her own." He held out his hands. "She was always transparent."

"That's actually a good trait for a person to have."

Brian nodded. "She has a lot of good traits."

"I'm sure she thought she was doing the right thing by keeping her thoughts to herself. So now we need to figure out how to lighten things up with David and get you and Kimberly on the same track."

"Without upsetting anyone," Brian added.

Pastor Rawlings shook his head. "I don't think it's possible not to upset anyone, but that's okay." He offered a sympathetic smile. "We're human. We get upset."

"I'm sure you're right." Brian started to stand but sat back down when the pastor bowed his head.

"Dear Father, in Your holy wisdom, please lead Brian, David, and Kimberly closer to You as they make life-affecting decisions. I pray for peace as well as healing of hearts that are surely broken. Give me the wisdom to offer advice when needed and the knowledge to know when to be quiet and let Your will show itself in a way only You can do. In Jesus' name, amen."

Brian whispered, "Amen," before opening his eyes.

Pastor Rawlings stood first, so Brian followed. Without another word, they shook hands, and Brian left the church.

The pastor's prayer played through Brian's head all the way home. He needed to rely more on prayer and less on his own will.

❧

Kim paced then flopped down on the couch where she couldn't sit very long without starting all over again. She'd been trying to call Brian, both at home and on his cell phone, for the past hour. She knew he'd already left work, because she'd tried there after not reaching him the first couple of times she called.

When her phone rang, she jumped. She paused long enough to look on the caller ID and saw that it was Brian. Her heart pounded, and her mouth suddenly felt dry.

As soon as she answered, Brian spoke. "What is going on, Kimberly?"

She swallowed hard, but the lump stayed at the base of her throat. "I had a talk with David."

"Yes, I know."

"I told him I couldn't marry him." Her hand shook, so she cradled the phone between her shoulder and ear.

"What else did you tell him?"

He sounded strange. "Do you already know?"

"Yes," he replied softly. "He said you told him you were in love with me. Why did you do that?"

Kim's knees felt weak, so she stepped across the room and

sat down on a kitchen chair. "Because—well. . ." It was hard to tell her best friend something that would change their relationship for good. She sighed. "Because it's true."

"Why am I always the last to know stuff like this?" Brian asked.

"Are you mad?"

"Mad? No. Why should I be mad?"

"So what did David say after that?"

Brian snorted. "He was furious. But I think he's fine now, after we met face-to-face at the church."

"So that's where you've been. I've been trying to get ahold of you since you left work."

"I turned off my phone." A brief pause fell between them before he spoke again. "You and I need to have a heart-to-heart talk, Kimberly Shaw. This is a serious matter that needs to be resolved before David leaves for the next mission."

"It's over between David and me, Brian," Kim said. "You and I can deal with our own issues after he's gone."

"That brings up another point."

"What's that?"

"Do we have issues?"

Kim sucked in a breath and blurted, "I think we do."

"Then let's talk about them."

"Not on the phone," she said. "Why don't you come over here, and we can discuss them in person."

"I'll be there in ten minutes."

After they hung up, Kim ran to her room and changed into something a little more flattering than the jeans and T-shirt she'd put on after work. Then she brushed her hair until it gleamed.

The instant the doorbell rang, Kim flung it open. He reached for her, pulled her into his arms, and lowered his face to hers for the most heart-stopping kiss she'd ever experienced.

seventeen

Brian hadn't planned the kiss. It just happened.

When he opened his eyes as he took a step back, he saw that Kim was just as stunned as he was. Without a word, he followed her into her house and all the way to the kitchen.

She turned to face him. "I figure we're better off in here because the lighting is better."

"Uh-huh." Nothing more intelligent than a simple grunt entered Brian's mind. He needed some time to recover from the kiss.

"I'm really sorry I messed things up between you and David," she said. "I know you were best friends and all, but..." She lifted her hands and let them fall back to her sides. "I knew I couldn't stay engaged to him, and I felt like I needed to explain why I was giving him his ring back. It just came out, and by the time I realized what I'd done, it was too late."

Brian took a step closer to Kim and placed his hands on her shoulders. "I understand. You didn't do anything wrong."

"But—"

He gently touched her lips with his finger. "Shh."

Kim nodded and blinked then smiled. "So what are we gonna do now?"

His heart flipped a little, causing him to pause before speaking. "I guess we need to see how you and I are as a couple."

She lifted her eyebrows. "A couple?"

He nodded. "Yes. That is, if you want to."

"A couple," she repeated. "You and me." A giggle came out of her beautiful, bow-shaped lips. "That sounds so—I don't know..."

"Wonderful?"

Her cheeks reddened, and she nodded. "Well, yeah."

"So what now?"

Kim shrugged. "I guess we should start dating or something."

"Ya think?" His tone came out teasing, and she looked stricken, so he added, "I agree."

Brian felt a sense of peace as she smiled at him. Then he remembered David. "We need to be very careful about how we handle this."

Sadness washed over her face. "I know. I never meant to hurt him."

"David's a strong guy, so he'll be fine. But you're right. We need to be very careful with how we show our new relationship to the public." He gently stroked her cheek with the back of his hand. "We have to be respectful."

&

Kim wanted to kiss Brian again, but she agreed that they needed to take their relationship slowly, even in private. After being engaged to the wrong man, she didn't want to make the same mistake twice. The chemistry was certainly there, and she liked everything about Brian. However, she needed to be sure that the excitement from changing their relationship didn't fade into a dull regret.

"I have to get to the office early tomorrow morning, so I need to run," Brian said as he edged toward the door. "Let's plan to see each other Friday night. Maybe we can rent a movie and watch it at my place or yours."

She nodded. They didn't need to flaunt their relationship to the world—especially since David was still in town.

The rest of the week seemed to drag. By the time Friday night rolled around, Kim was so happy she felt like she could jump out of her own skin.

They'd decided to watch the movie at Brian's house. When Kim arrived, she was greeted by a smiling man and the aroma of homemade chili.

"I feel like a princess," she said. "This kind of thing only happens in fairy tales."

Brian leaned down and dropped a quick kiss on her lips. Her knees instantly felt rubbery, but she managed to make it to the nearest chair.

"Want to eat first or start the movie?" Brian asked.

"Let's eat while we watch the movie," she replied. That way, they would have something to do besides kiss.

Brian grinned. "Good idea. Help me set up some TV trays."

They were halfway through the movie when the phone rang. Brian frowned, but he put the movie on pause. "I'll get off the phone as fast as I can."

Kim noticed that Brian paused after looking at the caller ID. When he picked up the phone and answered, his voice cracked. She sat and watched him as he listened before saying, "Uh-huh, that's great." He got quiet again then added, "I'm sure she'll be perfectly fine with that. Would you like for me to talk to her first?"

After Brian hung up, he turned to Kim with a wide smile. "That was David. You'll never guess what he just told me."

"What did he say?"

"He called Mercedes, and they're now dating. After you broke up with him, he ran into her at Blossom's. They started talking, and before he knew what hit him, she asked if she could go to his place and fix dinner."

Kim tilted her head. "He called to tell you that?"

Brian planted his fists on his hips, and the smile never left his face. "He called to ask if you'd be okay with him bringing Mercedes to church on Sunday."

"Wow." As Kim thought back to the night they were all together, she wasn't surprised. "David and Mercedes did seem to have quite a bit in common." She snickered. "He didn't waste any time, though, did he? Well, I'm glad he's not sitting at home seething."

"I think this changes things for us, too, Kimberly." Brian sat down next to Kim and placed his arm around her. "Would you like to go to church with me on Sunday—I mean as my—um, girlfriend?"

She laughed and nodded. "I thought you'd never ask."

"You will be okay seeing David with Mercedes, right?" Brian looked her in the eye.

"Of course, but I have to admit it'll seem a little weird."

"I know what you mean." Brian turned back to the TV. "Let's finish watching this movie. I have to go to the office in the morning, so I can't stay up too late."

⁂

Since Brian had to leave straight from church on Sunday to help a friend move, Kim agreed to meet him in the pew. They figured that would also feel less awkward if they ran into David and Mercedes on their way in. Kim arrived early to save a spot. She kept turning around to watch for Brian, who slipped in with five minutes to spare.

"Before you ask," he whispered, "I saw David and Mercedes in the parking lot. She didn't look happy about something."

"I wonder what," Kim said.

"Couldn't tell, but don't worry about it."

The music started, so they turned their attention to worship God. After church was over, Brian took Kim's hand and led her to the fellowship hall for Bible study. David and Mercedes stood outside the door of the big room, deep in discussion. Brian cleared his throat as they walked by.

David glanced up and did a double take. Kim felt awkward as she smiled at David first then Mercedes, who broke into a very wide grin.

"Hey, Kim!" Mercedes said a little too loudly. "I want to talk to you. Is there someplace we can get away for a few minutes?"

Kim glanced at Brian, who nodded. "Bible study doesn't start for another fifteen minutes. I'll save you a seat."

Mercedes looked at David, who nodded and said, "Why

don't you go outside and talk to get away from all the ears?"

Kim bristled. David still liked to be in control and tell people what to do. She turned to Mercedes. "Where would you like to go?"

Mercedes pointed to the exit door. "Let's go outside. I don't want to start anything with David's friends."

As soon as they were out the door, Mercedes stopped and turned to Kim. "Thank you so much for being understanding about David and me. He was worried you'd be upset."

"Why would I be upset?" Kim asked.

"After he dropped you off that night we went bowling, I called him, and we talked for hours." Mercedes let out a dreamy sigh. "I was crazy about him, but he's loyal to a fault." She paused. "I want to assure you that nothing happened between us."

Kim folded her arms and chuckled. "Oh, I believe you."

"I know he wanted Brian and me to hit it off, but he's just not my type. I hope he's not too heartbroken."

Obviously, David hadn't told Mercedes all the details. "I think Brian is just fine. In fact, he would probably be the first to give you his blessing to be with David."

"Oh good." Mercedes cast a nervous glance over her shoulder. "Now I have a really important question to ask. I'm way overdressed for this church. It's been a long time since I've stepped foot in a place of worship, so I feel totally dorky and out of the loop. I didn't know it was okay to wear pants in front of God. Is there any way you and I can—well, you know—get together, so you can fill me in on all the latest God stuff? I'm thinking about moving here permanently, and I really want to fit in."

Kim had to bite the insides of her cheeks to keep from laughing. She nodded, and when the urge to laugh subsided, she said, "I'd love to talk about the gospel sometime."

"Since you're a hairdresser, maybe I can book an appointment, and we can talk then." Mercedes patted her hair. "I've been doing it myself for the past year because—well, finances have been rather tight lately."

Kim rummaged around in her handbag and pulled out a card. "Give me a call, and we can set up an appointment. Your first visit is free." She was so relieved not to have to worry about David being mad at Brian, she would have given Mercedes more if she'd asked.

Mercedes nearly fell off her stilettos. "You'll do that?"

With a grin, Kim nodded. "Just call me early next week, and we'll find a time you can come in."

"You're a very sweet person, Kimberly. I think we just might wind up being best friends."

Kim had her doubts, but she wasn't about to tell Mercedes that. "Let's go back inside, okay? I think you'll enjoy the Bible study."

"I hope so. To be honest, it kind of scares me. Will someone call on me and, like, expect me to know stuff?"

"No," Kim replied. "It's actually the opposite. So many people want to talk, you have to really be on your toes to get a word in."

Mercedes visibly relaxed as they walked inside to join David and Brian, who'd saved them seats between them. Kim shared her workbook with Mercedes, who appeared to take everything in.

After the Bible study was over, Mercedes invited everyone to her place for brunch. Brian immediately said he had plans to help his friend move. Kim didn't want to hurt her feelings, and she didn't want to make things any more awkward than they already were.

"That sounds nice," Kim replied. "What can I bring?"

Mercedes touched her manicured finger to her chin. "How about juice? I have orange juice, but David said he prefers apple or grape."

That was the first Kim had ever heard this about David, making her think she might not have known as much about him as she thought. "Okay, I'll bring both. How many people are coming?"

Mercedes shrugged. "I'm not sure. David invited a few people, but we don't have a count. Good thing I bought a bunch of muffins and bagels."

"Hey, Kim, I gotta go," Brian said.

Mercedes handed Kim a card. "Here's my uncle's address. It's really easy to find."

"See you in a little while," Kim replied.

Brian walked Kim to her car and held the door while she got in. Then he leaned over and whispered, "Mind if I stop by your place after I'm done?"

"That'll be great!"

"How long do you think you'll be at your new best friend's brunch?" Brian quirked a smile that Kim tried to ignore.

"Not long."

He pushed back from her car. "I didn't think so. I'll have my cell phone on me, so call if you need me, okay?"

"I can't believe this is happening. It feels sort of strange."

"One of the things I love about you, Kim, is your ability to look past yourself and see someone else who needs to hear the gospel."

Kim left the church parking lot and stopped off at the grocery store. With four bottles of juice, she took off for Mercedes' uncle's house. All the way there, she did some mental role-playing about how to talk to David. The problem was she didn't have any idea how he'd act toward her.

The second she pulled into the parking space in front of the address, she spotted David coming toward her. "Kim! I'd like to have a word with you before you go inside."

"Okay." She pulled the bags from the passenger seat and got out.

He cleared his throat as he studied her face. When he spoke, his voice cracked. "Kim, I want you to know that I've thought about us."

She braced herself for anything. "David, I—"

"Give me a chance to tell you what's on my mind. I can't say I blame you now that I've thought it all over. At this point in my life, I'm not good husband material, so I think this is for the best. When I met you, I got all caught up in the way you lived your life. I'd never met any other woman so committed to her faith. You're a good woman, Kimberly Shaw, and Brian is a fortunate man."

She glanced down to hide her embarrassment before looking back at him. "Thank you, David."

"You did the right thing."

"I appreciate your understanding."

He took one of the bags from her and pointed toward the house. "Ready to face a roomful of people?"

"Ready as I'll ever be," she replied. "Let's go in."

Several people seemed confused, but David pulled a couple of the guys aside and explained what happened. Mercedes appeared oblivious to everyone and everything but David, whom she openly adored. Kim found herself feeling bad for Mercedes, until she got everyone's attention for an announcement.

After all eyes were on Mercedes, she grinned at David then turned to everyone else. "I've been thinking about going back to college for the longest time. When I told David, he encouraged me to go for it, even after I said I was too old."

"You're never too old to follow your dreams," David said.

"I have two years left to get my nursing degree, and I'm going for it!" She pumped her fist into the air, eliciting a round of applause from everyone in the room.

Kim saw the sparks between David and Mercedes, and that gave her a very good feeling. When she had a chance to turn her back without being conspicuous, she shut her eyes and softly said, "Thank You, Lord."

As soon as she was able to get away without being rude, Kim went home. Brian was in her driveway waiting for her. She ran straight to him.

He wrapped his arms around her waist, and she placed her hands on his face. "I think we should have thought about getting together a long time ago," he said. "Life would have been much simpler."

"Maybe," she said, "but we might never have appreciated what we have."

"True," he agreed. "The Lord's timing is much better than ours." He leaned down and dropped a quick kiss on her lips. "Wanna tell me how things went at the brunch?"

"Later," she said. "But right now I want another kiss."

☙

As soon as Jack's furniture was in place, he handed Brian a soft drink. "So tell me, when are you gonna propose to Kim?"

Brian chuckled. "What makes you think I'm going to propose?"

Jack chuckled. "You're a smart man. You're not about to let her get away again."

"You're right. I thought I'd do it soon."

"Good idea."

Brian finished his drink and tossed the can into the recycling bin. "Enjoy your new house, Jack."

☙

First thing Monday morning, Kim walked into the Snappy Scissors feeling all giddy. Jasmine glanced at her, turned away, then snapped back around. "I see you had a good weekend."

"Yeah, it was great."

Jasmine gave her a told-you-so smile. "See? Brian was the man for you all along."

"I should have listened to you," Kim admitted. "But oh well. At least we're together now."

"Don't let him get away," Jasmine said. "If he makes any sounds about making this relationship permanent, you'd better jump."

Kim laughed. "You don't mince words, do you, Jazzy?"

"Why should I?" Jasmine picked up the towel hanging on

the back of the chair and shook it out. "I'm old enough to know what I want and go after it."

"Me, too," Kim said.

The day was busy, which was good, because it flew by. Kim had just picked up her handbag from the back room when her cell phone rang. It was Brian.

"Hey, wanna go for a drive and grab some dinner in a little while?" he asked.

She closed her eyes and allowed the contentment to fill her soul. "Sure, sounds good."

"I'll pick you up in half an hour if that's okay with you."

"Okeydoke. I'll be ready."

ঽৄ

This was it. The big moment of reckoning. His nerves were on edge as he headed straight for Kim's place. She was standing at the door waiting for him.

"You look beautiful," he said as he gave her a hug.

"Thanks." She pulled back and winked. "So do you."

"Hungry?"

"Always."

Brian laughed. "Then let's go." They passed the jewelry store on the way to the restaurant. If everything went as planned, they'd be there before the night was over.

Kim ordered first; then Brian told the server what he wanted. Kim kept tilting her head and giving him an odd look.

"Why do you keep doing that?" he asked.

"You're acting strange."

Brian opened his mouth then shut it. He grinned.

"Okay, what gives?"

He glanced down at the table then looked back into her eyes. He'd hoped to do this in a more romantic setting, but anywhere he was with Kim was romantic, so he figured he might as well let her know what was on his mind.

"I love you, Kim."

"I love you, too, Brian."

"I was wondering. . ." He paused and made a face.

Her eyebrows shot up, and she leaned forward with her hands on the table. "Out with it, Brian. What were you wondering?"

He reached for her hands and held both of them. "How do you feel about spending the rest of your life with me?"

Kim closed her eyes, and when she opened them, he saw the tears. "Absolutely, yes!"

epilogue

Six months later, Kim and Brian said their wedding vows. When it was time to walk out of the church as husband and wife, Kim glanced over her shoulder at Mercedes. "Be ready," she mouthed.

Mercedes gave her a thumbs-up. "I'll be front and center."

Brian gave her a confused look. "What was that all about?"

"I'll tell you all about it later."

After they got outside, and people closed in on them, Carrie found her way to Kim's side. "I'll be standing over to your right. Just look at me, and I'll let you know where she is."

"Huh?" Brian tilted his head and gave Carrie a questioning glance.

Carrie laughed. "I figured if she catches the bouquet, it'll at least get him thinking." She gently pushed Kim and Brian toward the waiting limo. "Better get going so we can start the party."

Brian snorted as people continued to wave and blow bubbles when they passed. "Promise you won't tell, and I'll let you two in on a little secret."

"You've been keeping a secret from me?" Kim teased as Carrie helped her fold the bridal dress train into the car.

"Just this one."

"C'mon, Brian," Carrie urged. "Spill it so we can get this show on the road."

Brian winked at Kim then announced. "David's been looking at rings."

"Good!" Kim wriggled her eyebrows. "All the more reason she has to catch the bouquet. She's next!"

"Better her than me," Carrie said. "I'll run interference and make sure she gets it."

After she turned and walked away, Brian pulled Kim toward him and dropped a kiss on her nose. "I love you, Mrs. Estep."

A Letter To Our Readers

Dear Reader:

In order that we might better contribute to your reading enjoyment, we would appreciate your taking a few minutes to respond to the following questions. We welcome your comments and read each form and letter we receive. When completed, please return to the following:

Fiction Editor
Heartsong Presents
PO Box 719
Uhrichsville, Ohio 44683

1. Did you enjoy reading *Special Mission* by Debby Mayne?
   ❏ Very much! I would like to see more books by this author!
   ❏ Moderately. I would have enjoyed it more if

   _____

   _____

   _____

2. Are you a member of **Heartsong Presents**? ❏ Yes ❏ No
   If no, where did you purchase this book? _____

   _____

3. How would you rate, on a scale from 1 (poor) to 5 (superior), the cover design? _____

4. On a scale from 1 (poor) to 10 (superior), please rate the following elements.

   ____ Heroine   ____ Plot
   ____ Hero   ____ Inspirational theme
   ____ Setting   ____ Secondary characters

5. These characters were special because? _____

_____

_____

6. How has this book inspired your life? _____

_____

_____

7. What settings would you like to see covered in future **Heartsong Presents** books? _____

_____

_____

8. What are some inspirational themes you would like to see treated in future books? _____

_____

_____

9. Would you be interested in reading other **Heartsong Presents** titles? ❑ Yes ❑ No

10. Please check your age range:
   ❑ Under 18   ❑ 18-24
   ❑ 25-34   ❑ 35-45
   ❑ 46-55   ❑ Over 55

Name _____

Occupation _____

Address _____

City, State, Zip _____

E-mail _____

Heart♥ng

HEARTSONG PRESENTS TITLES AVAILABLE NOW:

Presents

Great Inspirational Romance at a Great Price!

Heartsong Presents books are inspirational romances in
contemporary and historical settings, designed to give you an
enjoyable, spirit-lifting reading experience. You can choose
wonderfully written titles from some of today's best authors like
Wanda E. Brunstetter, Mary Connealy, Susan Page Davis,
Cathy Marie Hake, Joyce Livingston, and many others.

When ordering quantities less than twelve, above titles are $2.97 each.
Not all titles may be available at time of order.